Sanford, James E.

Nuclear war diary

NUCLEAR WAR DIARY

by

JAMES E. SANFORD, JR.

EDITOR
Frank Alexander

TEXT ARTIST
James E. Sanford, Jr.

COVER ARTIST
Dawn Bates

FRONT ROW EXPERIENCE

Dedicated

to

Janelle and Justine

ABOUT THE AUTHOR

James Sanford's writing is as interesting as his life story. A high school drop out who returned from the Vietnam War and used his G.I. benefits to go to college and get an M.A. Degree at California State University, Chico. Since 1975 he has been a teacher and a free-lance writer. While teaching courses in Art, English, Poetry, Psychology and Social Science, Mr. Sanford has used his personal experiences to write articles about scuba diving for treasure, gold mining, jewelry making, war, antiques and travel. From 1981 to 1983, Mr. Sanford taught at San Quentin State Prison in California, where he worked with inmate artists to create murals, stain glass projects, and poetry for publication.

As a teacher at Liberty Union High School in Brentwood, California, Mr. Sanford works in the Alternative Education Program with students who may be in danger of becoming drop outs, like himself. He loves working with individual students and developing special reading projects to stimulate interest. This book is a result of working with young readers. Mr. Sanford believes that travel and experience broaden the mind, but reading is the next best thing.

PREFACE

Since 1945, the world has lived under the threat of nuclear destruction. Over the past twenty years, the potential for destruction of our world from the "Greenhouse Effect", a diminishing Ozone layer in our atmosphere, and ever increasing pollution, has become a growing concern. Entire subcultures and protest movements have developed around the desire to end the fear of worldwide holocaust. Unfortunately, governments don't always listen to their citizens, and not all citizens are aware of the potential for mass destruction that exists. Even in this era of "Glasnost", the spectre of worldwide conflagration lurks in our subconscious minds.

It would be easy to ignore the many possibilities that exist for planetary annihilation. Easier still to believe that government leaders, around the world, are intelligent, competent people, with our best interests in mind, who would never do anything to push the world over the edge, to destruction. However, history has shown that one man, one country, one event, can trigger a situation that can escalate out of control.

Man has very little control over other countries and their citizens, and even less control over nature. The world is constantly reminded of nature's dominance over us. Typhoons, hurricanes, earthquakes, volcanoes, floods, and droughts, are all samples of nature's power. It only takes one natural disaster, or man-made accident, to set off a chain reaction that could have irrevocable repercussions.

CONTENTS

JANUARY 18

My name is Jessie Tineford. I am (was) a ninth grader at Park Junior High School in Antioch, California. Three weeks ago there was a nuclear war. We are living and hiding in the old coal mines in the hills above the town of Antioch. Altogether there are six of us. My father, Gene, my mother, Ann, and my three sisters, Jamie, Nellie, and Jackie. My stepfather never made it home. My father came to our house and took my mother, his ex-wife, and us children to the safety of the mines.

It is three weeks since the war started and ended, I guess. It was the day after my fifteenth birthday, maybe my last. I don't know who was at fault, or who started it. The only thing certain is that at noon three weeks ago special news reports started coming in about escalating hostilities in the Middle-East. By six in the evening we were headed for shelter. It was about thirty minutes after we entered the old coal mines above town that the explosions started. The earth shook and reshook for the rest of the night. My sisters and I cried. Some of the mine tunnels caved in and a lot of dust filled the cavern we were in.

My father has said we may be the last survivors of the human race. He has told us that if we live through the next three months, we have a good chance of survival in whatever is left of the world. He says the world we knew is gone and things will never be the same. He suggested that I keep a diary. He takes me aside a lot and gives me advice and ideas. He says that being the oldest puts a lot of responsibilities on me. We have all been given chores to do in the caves. One of my duties is to write this diary. Somehow it seems dumb. No one will ever read it.

JANUARY 19

I think it is late in the afternoon. I have lost track of time. When I'm not teaching my sisters math and

English lessons, or helping mom prepare food, I'm sleeping.

Dad and I sat by the fire for hours last night. We talked about when we go out of the cave. He tried to explain what he thought we might find and the difficulties we might encounter. He scared me.

The thought of everything destroyed and all the people dead is very scary, but the thought of people burned by radiation and the other forms of suffering I might see, scares me more. Dad says there will be little or no safe food to eat or water to drink. He believes the few people who have survived will be like animals. I am very scared.

JANUARY 20

We are very lucky. Dad and I did some exploring in the caves. We found some fresh water in some of the lower caves. Dad thinks this water will be safe to drink. The water there now was underground when the war started. Water that seeps into the caves in the future will have to filter down through limestone rock. This may remove some of the radioactivity. The water we brought with us was getting real low. Now we may have an unlimited supply. I never thought I'd get excited about finding water.

JANUARY 22

My sister, Nellie, has been throwing up. Mom and dad aren't sure if it's radiation sickness or the change in our diets. She seems to be the only one affected. Dad has her separated from us in case it's something contagious. He says we are weakened by inactivity, diet, and a lack of fresh air. It will be more difficult for us to fight off illness.

I have been teaching my little sister, Jamie, how to

read. She is only three years old, but she is really smart. She's really cute, too. I love the way she walks around the cave giving everybody hugs and saying, "It's okay." She is my stepsister. She looks more like my stepdad than Nellie or I. I wonder if my stepdad survived the bombs. I wonder if anyone did? I feel really empty when I think all my friends, my relatives, and probably my stepfather, are all dead. It also bothers me to think that my sisters will grow up never knowing the little things that I've always just accepted as minor—little things like McDonald's hamburgers, Saturday night movies with your friends, Taco Bell's Taco Salad, slumber parties, watching soaps on television, going shopping, going to school. They will never get to do those things. Neither will I.

JANUARY 25

Unreal! Dad woke us all up this morning and made us do exercises. He says we have to get in shape for our health and to get ready to go outside. We did calisthenics and isometrics for over an hour. I'm already sore.

Mom and dad have been having some hairy old arguments. It reminds me of when they were still married. Sound really carries in here. I can always hear what they say. Today mom was saying she didn't want dad to treat us kids like soldiers. Dad told her the only way we'd all survive outside the caves if we are trained to act like soldiers. They fought for two solid hours. It's kind of nice to know that even a nuclear war can't change everything.

JANUARY 27

I'm so stiff I can barely move. Dad is putting us through Marine Corps boot camp. He was in the Marines. He went to Vietnam and did something called Force Recon. He says when we leave the safety of the caves we will have to fight to survive.

I would like to take this time to describe our present home. Set in the lovely rolling hills of East Contra Costa County, this rustic, multilevel, single family unit has spacious living quarters. High ceilings, cathedral-like passageways, and cavernous rooms are the main features of this country estate. Sand floors, simulated limestone/sandstone walls, constant cold air, and cold running water are just a few of the less than modern conveniences. Situated in a former Regional Park District and now in a high demand air raid zone, this lovely dwelling can be purchased with a few MX missiles down.

It amazes me that I can still have a sense of humor. I live with five other people in a set of four connecting cave chambers. Each measures about eighteen by thirty feet. Each is connected by a passageway ten to fifteen feet long and no more than six feet across, eight feet high. Nellie, who's eight, and I, sleep in one cavern. Mom, Jamie and Jackie, sleep in another. Dad sleeps in the main cavern we jokingly call the living room. Dad has carved a fireplace in one wall. We cook our food there. We have a lot of old dead wood we've collected from throughout the mines. We also have an unlimited supply of coal. These mines had produced coal from the 1860's to the turn of the century. When the coal wasn't profitable anymore, the mines exported the extremely fine sand to Europe to make glass.

The mine area was turned into a park for hiking, horseback riding, picnicking, and historical events. My dad used to bring my sister Nellie and I here on weekends when he visited us. It was so pretty then——covered with scrub Pines and Manzanita. There were birds, deer, raccoons, squirrels, and horses. I can't imagine how it looks now. It makes me very sad.

JANUARY 29

The living room is closest to the main tunnel we used

to enter the mines. We are probably three hundred yards from the entrance. The main tunnel has a lot of twists, turns and false shafts leading away from it. Last night, while we were all asleep, dad heard noises in the tunnels. He isn't sure what it was, but we are all on a strict silence alert. We brought two shotguns and two hunting rifles that belonged to my stepdad. Dad has a big pistol that he keeps with him at all times. Mom has a shotgun and is watching the back of the caverns. I have a shotgun and am sitting in the living room. Dad has left to go to the entrance. He says for us to shoot first, talk later. I'm scared.

SAME DAY

Dad was gone a long time. The girls were really good. They thought it was a game. Nellie watched Jackie and kept her quiet. I played softly with Jamie and she kept her voice to a whisper. I'm amazed at how mature Nellie is acting. She takes our whole situation totally serious. She is always asking dad really sophisticated questions. I don't know if she really comprehends the situation or just really enjoys the new amount of attention she is getting.

Dad says the tunnel is three quarters caved in near the entrance. Some animals had dragged in a partial cow carcass and had been eating it during the night. Dad says that was what he heard. He says he booby trapped the entrance so that we would hear if anyone tried to enter the mines. He told me that tomorrow he and I are going back in the mines to see if there are any other entry points we should close or booby trap.

JANUARY 30

I feel very sick right now. I don't know how else to say it. I threw up earlier, but my stomach is still upset.

Dad and I found two bodies. We went out early this morning (it's morning when we wake up) and walked way back in the mines. We found some mushrooms growing in one tunnel and brought some back to see if we can eat them. A little later we found a corpse. It was horrible. There was an air shaft to the surface that was mostly caved in. This guy had tried to climb down and fell. Dad said his neck was broken, but it didn't matter. He had no hair; his eyes were all cloudy and burned; and his clothes were burned and filthy. He had big purple sores all over his face and arms. Dad made me look and pointed stuff out like he was back teaching his dumb science class at school. He pointed out that the eyes burned by looking at the nuclear bomb flash and the sores came from radiation sickness. He said it was merciful the man had fallen and died.

An hour later we found a second corpse; well, part of a corpse. It was near a tunnel that angled up to the surface. I couldn't see the entrance, but I could smell smoke. The corpse of a human, female I think, had been dragged inside the cave and eaten; dad said by small animals, as indicated by the small teeth marks in the flesh. Apparently a lot of small, burrowing animals had survived the bombs. Now they are having a hard time finding food. Dad said there is a chance they could mutate into carnivorous animals. I remember when I thought Bugs Bunny was cute. Now he seems kind of repulsive.

Dad and I buried the two bodies in the soft sand floors of the caves. Then we covered the graves with large sandstone rocks so they could not be dug up again. Dad says there are probably a lot of sick and injured survivors wandering the hills. Some may be seeking shelter; some just lost and confused. He says we have to avoid them at all cost. We did not even touch the two corpses. We used old tree branches to roll them into their graves.

FEBRUARY 2

Our first month in the mines has passed. We are alive and well. Our days are very routine. We get up when dad says it's morning. We all do about an hour of exercising and stretching. Mom has lost a lot of weight and is starting to look like she did when she was still married to dad.

After exercising, we fix a meal of beans and tortillas, or rice and tortillas. We wash it down with water. Occasionally, we get some orange juice crystals mixed in with the water. We also get vitamins each morning. I've lost a few pounds, too. I actually feel pretty healthy.

Jessie's Wall Drawing Of A Guitar Player

After we clean up from breakfast, I take Nellie and Jamie to our bedroom cave and teach them. Jamie is learning her ABC's and how to read. Nellie is learning how to spell, read and do multiplication and long division. We have a few books and some paper and pencils. Mostly we write in the moist sand with sticks. It's like using a chalkboard. The girls and I have been drawing pictures on the walls with pieces of coal. I drew a neat picture of a lifesize guitar player.

In the late afternoon we all sit by the fireplace in the cave wall and dad talks to us. He talks about many different things. Mostly, he talks about what it's going to be like when we leave the safety of the caves. Sometimes he talks about how it was before the war. He says we must never forget what we once had, how good it was and how easily we lost it all. I never thought of my father as a sensitive emotional person, but I notice the mist in his eyes when he talks about his friends, his parents, and how sorry he is that we will have to live in a world devastated by nuclear war. Sometimes I think he wants to say that he wishes we had never been born——that he had never had children. He seems very sad at times, but he always jokes and laughs and tries to keep our spirits high.

In the evening we have our meal. It is usually canned vegetables mixed with rice. We brought a lot of rice and beans and canned vegetables with us when we came to the caves. We have rationed the food, but it is getting low. I don't think we have enough to last three months. Dad hopes the mushrooms we found in the lower caves are edible. If they are, we will be able to grow more and eat them forever.

After dinner, dad makes me write in this diary. He tells the girls stories and plays with them. His stories are full of little messages about how to live and act. The girls are learning about radiation and contamination while listening to cute little stories.

Once in a while dad has us make things. Once we made a stack of torches from old branches and dried moss that grows in the cave. Another time, dad had us carve bowls and spoons from old Manzanita branches. One time he had us sharpening small branches into twelve inch long spikes. He used the spikes to make a booby trap in one of the tunnel shafts.

FEBRUARY 4

I never thought I could enjoy eating mushrooms. Before

the war you couldn't have paid me to eat a mushroom. Now I think they're just great. They add flavor to our bland diet and allow us to expand our simple menu. Mushroom soup is my favorite. Dad says with the addition of mushrooms to our food stores, we will be able to last for several months in the caves. He says the mushrooms will be a safe food source even after we move out.

FEBRUARY 5

Two important things happened today. One was that Nellie is completely well. It has taken her over two weeks to get over her illness. She got really weak because she threw up everything she ate. Dad says the mushrooms probably helped her a lot. She is eating regularly now. We all watch her after she eats to see if the food will stay down. It's like an event. After an hour or so, we all applaud her. It's like watching a movie with a happy ending. I was really worried about her.

Today we also started mapping the mines. Dad and I took Nellie and went exploring some of the tunnels we have avoided. We found more exposed coal deposits, some more fresh water, another type of mushroom, lots of dead wood, and a storage area that had been used by the Park Rangers when the mines were open for tours. In the storage area we found tools, nails, wire, lanterns, kerosene, some flashlights, batteries, picks, shovels, and oxygen masks and air tanks. The best find was a case of canned Cokes.

We brought most of the good stuff back to our tunnel. Dad had me draw a line map of where each tunnel led. I marked each exit, each air shaft, and each tunnel that was completely caved in. We avoid going too deep in the mines because of the dangerous gases that exist there. Dad has each of us memorizing the map. He says we each need to know where we are at all times. We need to be able to move through the tunnels quickly and know where and what our resources are.

FEBRUARY 8

We had a little celebration today. Dad let each of us have a can of Coke. He is trying hard to raise mom's spirits. I have heard her crying at night and I'm sure dad has, too! She doesn't smile much anymore and I hear her tell dad that she wishes she were dead. She told me if it weren't for us kids, she would go outside and die with everyone else.

I think the party helped a little. When Jamie burped from the Coke, we all laughed, even mom. Jackie didn't have any. Dad said that since she's a year old she wouldn't appreciate it and it may not be good for her. Mom called him a "fuddy duddy" and gave Jackie a taste of hers. Jackie slurped it and made a funny face. The bubbles tickled her nose.

Our little party was fun, but I feel uneasy. It's like the lull before the storm. I have a sense of impending trouble. I don't know why, but I'm worried.

FEBRUARY 10

After exercise and breakfast this morning, dad put us on silent alert. He told us he would be gone for a-while. He told mom to keep us all in the living room with guns loaded, some food packed, and ready to move to the storage area we had discovered if anything happened. He told mom something in private and then he left.

I took care of the kids while mom prepared two pillow cases with canned foods and water bottles. We all dressed in our warmest clothes and rolled up blankets to carry if we had to move. I kept running over the map of the tunnels in my mind. I knew exactly which mines to take and where all the cutbacks were to get us to the storage area quickly.

At least two hours passed before we heard the gun shots.

They were just hollow thuds in the tunnels, but we knew what they were. I looked at mom and she shook her head "no". We sat quietly for another hour. Jackie was restless. I think she sensed our anxiety. Finally I told mom that I should go look for dad. In a very calm, but commanding voice, she said for me to relax and be quiet.

Dad returned a short time later. He was very pale and trembling. He told mom to relax and put things back to normal. He told her he was going to take a bath and I was going with him. Mom almost freaked. So did I. None of us had taken a bath in over a month. After we discovered water in the lower caves, we were allowed to wipe off with a wet towel, but not bathe. He looked at mom and said he'd been outside and he needed to wash off any possible radiation. Mom said nothing.

Dad and I went to one of the smaller pools and he washed himself and his clothes with a bar of handsoap. He told me to move to the side of the tunnel and turn off my lantern. When I did, I was blind. It was pitch black. My eyes slowly adjusted. Where dad had just bathed was a faint green glow—not much brighter than the dial on a watch, but glowing. I heard dad say for me to look at him and see if he glowed anywhere. Neither he nor his clothes glowed.

We returned to our cave and prepared dinner. Dad told me to mark the water pool on my map. He said mark it "poisonous."

After dinner dad seemed calmer than when he had first returned. He sat in front of the fireplace and hugged Nellie and Jamie. I think he cried, too.

FEBRUARY 11

Dad spoke with me this morning. He told me it is worse outside than he imagined. He explained that he went to the entrance yesterday because he had heard small animals in the tunnels, close to our caves. He is afraid the animals might hurt us, or contaminate us. He said he went out of the entrance to see if he could block it from the animals coming in. When he got out of the cave he couldn't believe what he saw. Dad says everything is grey. The sky is dark grey. The ground is covered with a layer of grey dust, like snow. He says there are small packs of animals and large hordes of beetles and ants feasting on dead carcasses. Some of the carcasses are cows, horses, deer. Some are humans.

Dad said he did not go more than a few yards away from the main entrance, but as far as he could see everything that had been above ground was turned to dust. While he was out, two dust covered raccoons came towards him. He shot them both. Those were the shots we heard. He then returned to the caves and closed the entrance completely with dirt and wood. He says when we get ready to leave we can dig out the entrance!

FEBRUARY 13

We are back to routine. Not much going on. Dad has been explaining to mom that the devastation may be worse here than other places. He told her that this area was full of prime targets. To the south had been the Livermore Radiation Laboratory; to the east had been Rancho Seco Nuclear Power Plant and Stockton's shipping terminal. To the north had been Travis Air Force Base. To the very close west had been the Concord Naval Weapons Station and beyond that the Alameda Naval Air Station. In and around Antioch itself had been a half dozen major industries, including Dow Chemical, Dupont, and U.S. Steel. Dad explained that it was likely that more than two or three missile warheads fell in a very close proximity. That would account for the complete devastation in this area. He says that in some rural areas the damage may be considerably less.

It has been six weeks since we first entered the mines.

I'm getting curious about what the outside world is going to look like. As scary as it is, I still feel a sense of anticipation. At first I thought it might be better to have died in the first attack; now I'm glad I survived. I'm scared, but I'm not guilty or ashamed that I have survived. I really want to live and accomplish something in the new world. There must be a reason my family and I survived.

FEBRUARY 15

Today is mom's birthday. She is thirty-six years old. Her hair is still long and blond. Her eyes are still blue and clear and she doesn't have a lot of wrinkles. Since we've been in here she has lost about twenty pounds.

Dad borrowed some paper from my school tablet and drew a great picture of our house. It had trees and shrubs and said "Happy Birthday" from all of us. He gave it to her after breakfast. He told her that next year he'd get her a nice gift. She gave us all a hug and a kiss, then went to her room cave and didn't come out until dinner. I wish she wasn't so depressed. I feel helpless 'cause I can't do anything to help her or cheer her up. Dad says she'll be better when we can get out of the caves.

FEBRUARY 16

Nellie, dad and I went to one of the big caverns in the back of the mines and practiced killing. Dad taught us what every post-nuclear war female should know. First, he had us disassemble and assemble a rifle, a shotgun and his pistol. After each was back together he had us fire at a target shaped like a man. He says, "Never shoot at another human being unless you shoot to kill." He pointed out where to shoot the target, so that if it were a person it would kill. I did okay, but Nellie hates the guns. She did good with the shotgun. It's hard to miss someone at point blank range with a shotgun.

After the guns, dad showed us how to make Molotov cocktails with empty bottles and kerosene. He also taught us how to make pipe bombs with match heads or powder, and a piece of pipe. He told us how to make gun powder out of sulphur, charcoal and saltpeter. He told us where we would find such materials in an emergency.

When demolition school was over dad took out two pieces of wood shaped and carved like knives. They had no edge and the points were blunt. Dad showed us how to conceal a knife and how to kill with it. We used him as a practice dummy. He had Nellie and I practice coming up behind him and killing him by slitting his throat. He also taught us how to kill someone in a frontal assault. Nellie was hesitant at first, but dad told her she had to learn because someone might try to hurt her or one of our family. She tried harder after that. I know I'd have no trouble killing anyone who tried to hurt anyone in my family.

Dad also taught us some basic hand-to-hand combat moves. He gave us some kicks, punches and crippling blows to practice on our own. He says we will have occasional practice sessions in the future and we will continue our morning exercise program.

FEBRUARY 18

Dad must be getting restless. He has been talking more and more about going out and exploring. I'm feeling the same furtiveness. I guess I'm more like my dad than I know.

I find myself psyching up mentally for the day when I go out to face the new world! I'm taking my exercise periods seriously, and I practice weapons or self defense. I spend time thinking about what I'd do in different situations. I think I enjoy this military way of thinking.

FEBRUARY 20

Dad gave me hell today. I thought he was going to hit me. He really got pissed because I yelled at mom. She was raging on me because I was cleaning the rifles and telling Jamie I'd teach her how to shoot someday. I told her she'd better stop living in the past and get used to the way things are. I didn't know dad was around. He came flying out of the entrance tunnel and grabbed me by the neck. His face was about an inch from my face and he was really hot. He said if I ever spoke to mom like that again, he'd beat my ass until I couldn't sit down. Then he told me to go to my room and stay till dinner. I started to argue, but decided that I'd better keep my mouth shut. I'm in my room chamber waiting for dinner. Dad knows what I told mom was true, but he doesn't want us saying it to her face. I will have to watch what I say and do in front of her.

FEBRUARY 21

I think dad was feeling a little bad about jumping on me yesterday. This morning I told him I was low on writing paper. He told me he thought he saw some paper on a shelf in the storage area we discovered. He said he'd give me thirty minutes to go there, check, and get back. He actually let me go off in the mines by myself. He even gave me his pistol. It's a forty-four magnum. It's really heavy and it kicks worse than a shotgun.

I took the gun and an empty pillow case on my trip. There were some other goodies I had seen there and I wanted to bring them back. I left and traveled the quarter mile of tunnels in about five minutes. I took a flashlight instead of a lantern, so I could move faster. The light casts an eerie illumination in the tunnels. You can only see about fifty feet ahead and there are a lot of weird shadows. When I got to the storage area, I lit a lantern with mom's Bic lighter. The storage area sits at the junction in the sandstone wall. It goes back about twenty feet from the tunnel and is about twenty feet long. Across the front of the niche is a wood and

chicken wire fence with a gate in it. Just inside the
gate, against one wall, are four wooden shelves mounted
on the sandstone wall.

I went to the shelves and found an open box with four
unused yellow, lined tablets. I also found two new ink
pens in the box. I put the tablets and the pens into
my pillow case and went looking for the other items
I had been wanting to return for. In the back of the
storage area was a keg of nails. Sitting on top of the
nails was an old inner tube from a tire. I quickly put
it in my goodie bag. Behind the keg of nails, laying
on the sand floor was a number of three-eighths inch
steel dowels. Each was about twenty-four inches long.
I put four in my bag.

I returned to our cavern with plenty of time to spare.
Dad nodded as I entered the cave. He acted really
cool, but I could tell from mom's expression and dad's
posture that they had worried the whole time I was
gone. I tried to be equally nonchalant about my first
feeling of freedom in almost two months. I put my
little treasures in my room and said nothing about them.

FEBRUARY 22

I took a butcher knife, a hammer, a pair of pliers, a
metal dowel, and the rubber innertube, and I went a
ways back in the tunnels. It took two hours of bending,
cutting, and experimenting before I finished my proto-
type. I practiced with my homemade slingshot for an
hour. I returned to our cavern with my new toy hanging
from the back pocket of my jeans.

Dad knew I had been up to something since I got back
yesterday, but he hadn't said anything. As soon as I
passed him, he started laughing. Mom and Nellie couldn't
figure out why dad was laughing convulsively on the
sand floor. I stood by quietly, looking smugly at my
dad. When he had composed himself, he asked me to
let him see my invention. He looked at it admiringly.
He took a small stone from the floor and fired it down
the entrance tunnel. He giggled as he handed it back.

He said it may need a few modifications, but it was an excellent idea. He told mom he would never have thought of it. He showed me what changes to make and told me to make a couple more.

I feel like I've finally made a contribution to our family and our situation. I feel good right now.

FEBRUARY 24

Dad came back a little while ago from checking some new tunnels. He says the old shafts go for miles. He believes several go as far as the town of Clayton. That is about five or six miles from here. He told us that he thinks there are other people in the mines——possibly survivors who made it into the caves on the other side of the mountains. Dad says he heard sounds and saw signs of recent habitation. He didn't see any people.

FEBRUARY 25

Mom and dad have been arguing. Dad wants to take me and go check the mines to the west for other survivors. Mom doesn't think we should have contact with other people. She doesn't want to share what we have and she's afraid of violence. Also, mom doesn't want me going with dad and getting hurt. She doesn't think I can take care of myself.

Dad has asserted his position. Tomorrow he an I are going to make a long hike through the mines to the .west. We are going to look for survivors. We are going to observe, not make contact. We will have to traverse the tunnels that go deep inside the mountain that separates our mines from the mines that existed in the west. It is probably two miles. Dad says we will take a shotgun and his pistol.

FEBRUARY 28

In three days I have aged a lifetime. I have seen much and I am a lot older and wiser. I will never be a child again. I am now an adult, but I'm not sure why.

Dad and I traveled to the mines on the western side of the mountains. We found several open airshafts and two open entrances. We did not go outside the caves. At one entrance we heard a sound like growling. Dad went forward and I stayed back. I had the shotgun. It was loaded and I had the safety off.

After dad entered the tunnel to the entrance I heard a voice. My dad was talking to someone. I moved forward and peeked around the corner of the tunnel wall. Laying propped against the sandstone wall, near the entrance, was a woman. She was clutching a bundle to her chest. The lady was very sick. The growl we had heard was the lady vomiting. She was very dirty and she had lost most of her hair. She had big open sores on her face, neck and arms. The lady was pleading with my dad to help her baby. Dad examined the lady and the bundle, then I heard him speak to the lady in a very low, soothing voice. He told her her baby was dead and she was dying from radiation sickness. He explained that there was nothing he could do to help her. The lady began sobbing softly. After a moment she asked my father to kill her. Dad hesitated a moment, then he took out his pistol. He leaned close to the woman and was speaking very softly and soothingly. I saw him bring the gun up close to her forehead. She was weeping softly into the bundle at her chest. Dad slowly leaned away from the woman, but held the gun close to the woman's head. I pulled back from the corner and closed my eyes. I heard my father say, "May a merciful God help you find your baby on the other side." The gunshot was a small explosion that hurt my eardrums. I did not look to see the havoc wreaked by the bullet. I heard my dad burying the body. Twenty minutes later we resumed our trek. Dad was very calm and quiet as we traveled.

An hour later we were examining a large cavern that

had a dozen tunnels branching out and away from it. Dad took a piece of charcoal and numbered each of the tunnel entrances. As he approached one tunnel entrance, he froze. He turned and signaled me forward. As I came up behind him I heard voices. Somewhere down the tunnel, people were talking. More than two people were in a heated discussion. Dad whispered for me to stay behind and he moved into the tunnel. He came back after about fifteen minutes. He did not speak, he just signaled for me to follow. We entered the adjacent tunnel and moved quietly down the shaft. A hundred yards in, the tunnel ended, but there was an opening the size of a window. The opening looked into the next tunnel and was about ten feet above the floor of the other cave. From our vantage point, we could look and listen to the people there without being observed.

The cavern below was like a large meeting hall. In the center of the cavern was a large fireplace. There was a small bonfire burning and a dozen people clustered around it. On the sides of the cavern were small cubicles set up for individuals to sleep. Some of the cubicles had people lying in them. All in all, there were approximately two dozen men, women and children.

The group around the fire was discussing their present food shortage. One older man saying that he thought the group should send someone out to find food. He was shouted down by two younger men who said it was suicide to go out and there was no food anyway.

Another man, wearing a thick black trench coat, stood up next to the fire. When he stood, everyone else got quiet and stared at him. His voice was very rich and deep, and he spoke slowly and deliberately. He reminded the group that it had been his plan to come here and that he was still in charge. He told them that it was his intention to stick to their original plan. The strong and healthy would get their ration of food. The weak and sick would have to fend for themselves. If the weak and sick wanted to go out in search of food, they could follow Maryann and her dead baby. The big man squatted down next to the fire again and all but two men moved away to the cubicles at the side of the cavern.

Dad touched my shoulder and signaled for me to follow him out of the tunnel. We moved out to the large cavern with all the tunnel entrances. Dad led us back to the long mine shaft that led to our caves. We went about fifty yards into the shaft and stopped. Dad took something from his coat pocket and climbed a short ways up the tunnel wall. There was a large overhang of sandstone near the ceiling. I watched as dad placed a small bomb, made from bullet powder, in position. He signaled me to move further down the tunnel. I went another fifty yards and hid behind a big sandstone boulder. A moment later dad came running down the tunnel and slid down next to me behind the rock. We covered our ears. The small bomb exploded and I felt the concussion against my chest. It made my ears ring. We moved to where the blast had occurred. Three quarters of the tunnel, from the floor up, was caved in. Dad says there are other passages we may have to block later. We left and headed back to our side of the mountain.

We were almost back to the familiar tunnels of our mines when dad leaned closer to me and said we were being followed. He told me to keep walking, that he was going to fall back and find out who it was. I did as I was told, but I was scared. I walked another fifty or sixty yards, then I slipped into a false cave and waited. I put down my goody bag and kept only my flashlight and my shotgun. My wait lasted about ten minutes. I heard a scuffle back in the tunnel. I waited until it was over, then I moved quietly towards the voice I could hear. I turned my flashlight off and walked in total darkness. As I got close to where the voices were I could see the faint glow of another light. I peered in and I could see the back of a young man. As I inched closer I could see that the man was standing over dad with a flashlight and a gun. I braced myself against the wall and took aim at the back of the man's head. I didn't want to hit dad.

I screamed out in my deepest, harshest voice, "Freeze, asshole!" The man gave a sudden start, but he froze. He slowly raised his arms above his head. Dad stood up and took the man's flashlight and gun. They moved to where I was standing. I lowered the shotgun and turned on my light. The man was tall, slender, fair complexion, and apparently not contaminated by radiation.

Dad told him to put his hands down and have a seat on the cave floor. We interrogated him for an hour. His name was Harry. He had been a volunteer with the regional park district. His hobby was "spelunking." He had spent hundreds of hours exploring and mapping the mines for the park district. He had been in the mines the day the bombs fell. He didn't realize what had happened until he went above ground. Once he found out what had happened, he decided to stay in the mines. He knew about the water and mushrooms in the caves. He told us he had been in the lower mines about a week before he knew other people were there. He had avoided contact with the people because he feared contamination and violence. He knew about the group we had seen. He told us they were very cruel. There had been close to fifty the day after the war. Due to radiation, more than half had died. Their leader is a local doctor who brought the group here with promises of medical treatment and medicine.

We left Harry in the mines with an invitation to come visit and talk about the future. Harry told us he prefers to roam the caves on his own, but that he would come by and he would keep us informed about the other people in the mines.

We returned to our caves without further incident, but not without a lot of new feelings and emotions. Cruelty and death are the new terms for describing my world.

MARCH 1

Two full months in the gloom and cold of dark, dank mines is not good for physical or mental health. My eyes have become accustomed to reading, eating, and living in the light of lanterns, flashlights and cooking fires. The whole family has the pallor of corpses. The lack of sunlight has not only ruined our tans, but also depleted some very necessary vitamins. We take vitamin pills, but we aren't getting the vitamin C, D, and A we need. Dad and mom are worried about Nellie, Jamie and Jackie getting sick from scurvy, rickets or other illnesses. Our immunity systems are low and our environment is not made for good health. The cold and moisture are bad enough, but poor diet, sleeping on the ground, and lack of proper vitamins, makes us all prime targets for colds, flu and pneumonia. We all continue to do exercises each morning, but my strength is less than what it was and so is everyone else's. Both Nellie and Jamie are getting listless. They spend a lot of time sleeping. If for no other reason than sunlight and air, we will have to leave the caves soon.

MARCH 3

Good day today. Harry showed up before dinner. He stayed for dinner and a long talk afterwards. Harry and dad think a lot alike. They both have good minds and a great deal of information. Each of them has knowledge in different areas. Together they are a real storehouse of learning. When dad is weak in an area, Harry knows the subject. When Harry isn't sure about something, dad usually has the facts. They spoke about plans for some expeditions outside in the near future.

Dad made the girls, mom and I go to bed early. He and Harry talked for some time after. I think dad is happy to find another person to talk to and associate with. Even though Harry is only twenty-five and had never been in the military, he understands and agrees with dad's military thinking. I fell asleep trying to hear all that they were saying.

MARCH 5

Harry showed up today. He brought a three pound coffee

can full of meat chunks. He told us that there are wild boar living deep in the mines. He says we can go and hunt some if we like the meat. Dad says the meat will add some necessary protein and vitamins to our diet.

We cooked the pork at dinner and mixed it with rice. It needed salt or something, but it was good. The girls loved it and it made mom smile, too. Tomorrow Harry and I are going to go boar hunting. Dad told me to take my sling shot. He doesn't want to waste bullets, or attract attention to this part of the mines. He and Harry assure me that I can kill a boar with my sling shot. I'm really excited.

MARCH 6

I'm flabbergasted! Dad and Harry lied to me. They lied to all of us. Harry and I went into the mines this morning. We went to a deep shaft that was moist and moldy. Instead of hunting wild boar, I learned how to hunt big slugs and salamanders. After you catch them, you cut the heads off and fillet the big fat bodies. I captured about forty of them—just enough to make a three pound coffee can look like it was full of pork chunks. I brought them back and smiled at all the congratulations I got for being a great hunter. We all had another great meal of meat and beans. It was like a great chili feast. Dad, Harry and I all chuckled as mom and the girls munched down the meaty meal. I ate well, too. It's amazing how easy it is to eat gross things when you're hungry and you know it'll save your life. We are not going to tell mom and the girls about the meat. It'll make it easier for them to eat.

MARCH 8

Dad and Harry met today. They are planning a short excursion outside the caves. They are going to go out early in the morning, before sunrise. They want to be outside as daylight comes so their eyes will adjust slowly to the increased light. We have been underground for over two months. The only light we've used is flashlights, lanterns, and cooking fires.

Dad told me they are taking gas masks and that they are going to cover all exposed skin surfaces and try to seal their clothing against dust getting inside. The less radioactivity they are exposed to, the better.

I will accompany them to the exit they are going to use. I am to wait there until they return. They told me if anything should happen to them, I am to take care of mom and the girls. I wish I were smarter and braver.

MARCH 10

Harry and dad went outside this morning. I sat with them by a narrow cave entrance and watched the dim light of a heavily overcast day come into the mine opening. It is the closest I came to the outside. It was exciting sitting ten yards from the door to my new world. I stared hard at the small patch of gray sky I could see. I strained my ears to hear outside sounds.

My father and Harry returned about six hours later. They came into the entrance talking and breathing hard. The entrance they had chosen is high up on a hillside. To get to it they had to climb up at a very steep angle. It took them several minutes to catch their breath and relax. As they composed themselves, they made references to sights they had seen.

Shortly they both removed all their clothing and buried it in the sand floor. Dad's body has lost more than twenty pounds and is now as lean and hard as pictures I saw of him when he was young. Harry is ten years younger and healthy, but he doesn't have the thick muscles like dad.

Harry and dad carried their shoes, guns and gas masks back into the mines with them. They walked barefoot and naked through the mines to the water pool they used to bathe. After they washed themselves and their gear, they dressed in clothes they had placed there earlier.

Together we all returned to our caves. When we got there, mom fixed some food and we listened as dad and Harry described what they did and saw. They told us that they followed the ravine that used to be the road all the way to town. The buildings that used to be County East Mall are completely devastated, but there are survivors living within the ruined walls. Dad says it's probably for protection from the constant cold wind and also because there is food, clothing and other items to be scavenged.

Harry said from the mall area they could see all the way to the river. He told us that there are only skeletons of the factories and large buildings. The firestorm from the missile warheads burned everything in the area.

Dad says there is a layer of ash everywhere. In some places it's a foot deep. The wind keeps it stirred up and makes the air seem misty.

Both Harry and dad talked about looking for food and water. The few survivors have hoarded all the food they can find. There has been no rain since the war. Water is very scarce. Harry says they saw several large fires—not small cooking fires, but huge billowing plumes of black smoke. He thinks the fires are the cremation of dead people.

Mom asked them if they spoke with anyone. Dad said they talked to a girl about my age. He said she was scared by their appearance and seemed to be in shock. She suggested that they go to the Red Cross Station at Los Medanos College.

Harry said he spoke to an old man who was living in a large drain pipe by the road. When Harry asked about survivors the old man said they were either dead or dying. He told Harry that there are gangs of men and boys who raid food and water from the other survivors. He said they come at night when everyone's asleep.

Dad and Harry agreed that the majority of survivors they saw were in some stage of radiation poisoning. All had hair loss, teeth loss, and sores. Some sort of aid station had been set up at what had once been the local community college. Dad and Harry want to go there, but are not sure they should.

MARCH 12

Harry and dad have come to a decision. Harry is going to go outside alone. He is going to go to the college where the aid station is. Dad believes the officials there can give them information they need about radiation levels, food, water and survivors in other areas.

Harry is going out tomorrow morning. I am going to accompany him to the exit and wait for his return.

MARCH 14

It is late evening. I know because I watched the sunset on another overcast and gloomy day. That was at least four hours ago. Harry returned about thirty minutes after dark. He thought he had been followed. We sat by the entrance for an hour. We listened for sounds of other survivors who might be following Harry to our hiding place.

When we were certain no one was coming, Harry undressed and buried his clothes. We went into the mines and Harry bathed. We walked back to our caves then Harry gave me a hug and went off by himself. He is very quiet, but tonight he was really upset by something. He didn't talk at all. Harry said he would be around in the morning to talk to dad. I feel very sad and lonely. I feel sorry for Harry because he has one one.

MARCH 15

Harry and dad spent the morning talking privately. They got angry when I tried to join them. I feel uneasy about what Harry found out when he went outside yesterday.

SAME DAY

We had a family meeting awhile ago. Harry talked about his trip outside and what he found. He was very upset.

According to reports from survivors who came into the aid center at the college, everything to the west is gone. San Francisco, Berkeley, Oakland, Richmond, Concord, San Leandro, Hayward and San Jose don't exist anymore. The combination of missile warheads and fire completely obliterated everything above ground. Early reports said one out of every thousand persons survived. After the fallout and radiation took its toll, the figure became one in two thousand.

To the north, the information seemed a little more positive. Both Sacramento and Travis Air Force Base had been hit by missiles, but nothing further north. The National Guard and the Red Cross have established aid centers in Chico, Oroville, Redding, Ukiah, Corning and Fort Ross. Fallout has been the worst problem in the north, but there is food and water. South and east of us there have been little or no reports. Someone told Harry that Livermore Radiation Laboratory took two thermonuclear hits. Harry's parents lived in Livermore.

Two professors at the college have been monitoring radiation and fallout in this area. They told Harry that one contributing factor to survival in this area was low fallout. The northwesterly winds, common to this time of year, pushed the major fallout south before moving it inland. The bad news is that it was pushed into the fertile central valley of California. The majority of the state's agricultural land is now highly con-taminated.

The other bad news that Harry brought was about rain. There has been none in almost three months. The ash that has accumulated everywhere is radioactive and it continues to kill those who are exposed to it. The Red Cross estimates about twenty-five hundred survivors in Pittsburg, Antioch and Oakley/Brentwood. More than half are suffering from exposure to radiation. The levels of radiation outside are still too high for us to move out of the caves.

MARCH 18

It has been three days since the accident. Harry is dead. I am still sick and find it difficult to breathe deep without coughing. It is so ironic that the mines that have protected us and were so loved by Harry, became so dangerous. Harry knew these mines like an old friend. He was respectful of their protection and resources.

Three days ago Harry and I started down into the lower caves to get food. We were talking and laughing. It was the first time Harry had laughed since his return from the outside. He was saying we should corner the market on fresh slug meat. We had just climbed down one level and started into a tunnel when Harry stopped. He turned and yelled for me to run. I turned and raced back to the cutback at the next level. I could hear Harry right behind me. He kept saying, "Oh damn; oh shit!" I can't remember how long or how far I ran. I woke up here in the living room cave by the fire. The barometric pressure in the mines dropped. Deadly car-bon monoxide and methane gasses rose up from the lowest caves. I was overcome by the gas in small amounts. I have partial paralysis in my legs and some lung damage, but both will pass. Harry died. Dad say Harry was lying only fifty feet behind the spot where I was found unconscious.

Because of Harry we have survived longer than we could

have. He was a good, decent young man. If he had lived, he could have been a good leader when we go outside. Now, no one but this family will ever know of his goodness as a human being. The mines that saved him from the war took his life in peace. I miss him already. I think I loved him, but I'll never know.

MARCH 19

Dad, mom and I had a long talk earlier. Dad explained that he and Harry had made plans to begin moving outside. Harry's last report made it clear that we still could not live outside the caves with radiation levels still very high. Dad is proposing that we remain close to the mines and bring what we need here. As soon as I am well, he wants to take me and go looking for items we can use in the caves. Mom was surprisingly in favor of the idea. I think Harry's death in the mines has made her less dependent upon staying hidden here.

The three of us made a list of items that we felt would help our stay inside the tunnels. The list included cooking utensils, warm clothing, more blankets, soap, wash rags, towels, toilet paper, tooth brushes, combs, candles, matches, games, books and toys. The last three items were Nellie's idea.

The heaviness in my legs is leaving. My chest is not as sensitive either. Dad says going out and moving around will help to burn toxins out of my body faster. We are planning to go out day after tomorrow.

MARCH 20

Dad and I have made our final preparations. We will go out at sunrise tomorrow. We will use the same exit that dad and Harry used previously. I will wear Harry's clothes and gas mask. Dad has shown me how to tie down my pant legs and jacket sleeves to keep out as much ash and dust as possible.

We have fashioned backpacks out of pillow cases and handmade frames. We are taking out small bags of fresh mushrooms, rice, beans, and slug meat. Dad says we can bargain with uncontaminated food, but we must not flaunt it. People must not know where we got it, or where we come from.

Dad has sawed the barrel off my shotgun and cut the stock down. It is now only about eighteen inches long and easy to conceal. I have it loaded with five rounds of number three shot. At close range, it will kill. At a little distance it will stop, but not kill.

MARCH 22

Mom's worst fear came to reality. It happened while dad and I were outside yesterday. Suddenly the severity of our situation is more real to me. First, Dad and I had a confrontation with a gang of young survivors near the college. Then, we got back to the mines to find we'd been robbed. Two men came into our caves. They pushed mom around and took a box of canned vegetables. Nellie wounded one of the men with a knife before they got away. Mom was near hysterics when we got back. She says she and the girls are lucky to be alive.

Dad and I went to the college and bartered for some of the items on our list. Word got out fast that we had uncontaminated food. While dad spoke with the Red Cross people and some college professors about setting up a meeting to organize the survivors, a group of young guys set an ambush near the campus. I don't know what they actually wanted, because dad shot the leader as soon as he made his intentions known. There were ten guys, all about twenty years old. They were all scroungy and dirty. Most of them came out of the trailer of a burned-out semi truck. The leader said they were hungry and needed food. Dad told him we had food to trade. The leader pulled a big hunting knife out and told dad he had nothing to trade. He said he'd let us live if we gave him our food and whatever else we had. I never saw the gun. I just heard the cannon-like roar and saw the surprised look in the leader's eyes as the bullet almost cut him in half. I pulled out my shotgun and pumped a round into the chamber. The other young men froze. Dad took out our shopping list and handed it to a black kid who was staring at blood that had splattered on him. Dad told him to go out and find those items and take them to Professor Bronson at the college. He told them the next time we came we'd trade food and fresh water for those items. We left and came back to the mines. After we washed and changed, we went to our caves to find what had happened there.

Dad is really hot. He put mom to bed. He cleaned up the mess the two men had made of our food stores. He gave Nellie my sawed off shotgun and told her to shoot anyone entering the chamber. He gave me the other shotgun and loaded it with double ought shot. We left our chambers an hour after we arrived. We traveled through the mines to the caves in the eastern part of the hills. When we reached the tunnel that led to the cathedral cave where we had seen the other survivors, we split up. I went down the tunnel to the window cave, so I could cover dad. He went directly into the cavern of survivors. I reached my vantage point just in time to see dad striding into the cavern. He halted ten feet from where the survivors were clustered around the circular fireplace. The group was so intent on cooking up our canned vegetables they did not even notice dad.

"Who the hell is in charge of this band of thieves?" dad demanded in a loud, angry voice.

The group was so startled that some of them screamed and fell to the ground. After a moment, the big man in the dark coat stepped forward. It was the same voice I had heard before.

"I speak for these people. Who are you? the big man asked in a rather indignant voice.

Dad told him that he was the owner of the food they

were cooking. He told him that someone in his group stole the food.

The big man got angry. He started yelling at dad about food belonging to the one who possesses it——that his people needed it——that dad was a selfish monster who would rather see women and children starve than share. The group was agreeing with the big man and started calling dad names. Dad remained very calm. He spoke to the whole group. He told them he could teach them how to survive in the mines until it was safe to leave, but he would not tolerate anyone stealing his family's food. As he was speaking I saw two shadowy figures moving in a cubicle behind dad. They had clubs and were sneaking up behind him. I clicked off the shotgun's safety and took aim at the first figure. I aimed first at the chest, then I lowered my barrel and fired. The round hit the figure just above the knees. He fell sideways and lay on the floor screaming. When dad heard the shot, he pulled his pistol and leaped on the big man. He straddled the big man's chest and placed the barrel of his pistol in the man's throat. I could not hear what dad was saying, but the big man nodding "yes" to everything.

After several minutes, dad got off the big man and spoke to the group. He told them his offer to teach them still stood. He also told them to eat the canned vegetables, but to make sure that everyone got fed. Finally, he told the group that the big man was a sick, dishonest person who was only using them. He explained that they did not need a mean and vicious leader. Share and share alike, he said, or you will not survive long.

Vowing to return soon with food and water for them, he backed out of the cavern. When he was safely into the tunnel, I left my vantage point and went to meet dad.

We returned to our caverns through the long tunnels under the mountain. Dad and I sat by the fireplace for a long time without speaking. Finally, dad put his arm around my shoulder and spoke into the crackling fire. He said he was sorry the world was so screwed

up and that I had to live in a world of violence and suffering. All I could think of was how easy it would have
been to kill the man tonight, but I didn't.

MARCH 24

Dad came in this afternoon. He was all excited. He
was close to an airshaft and heard something weird.
He investigated and found that it is raining outside.
He says it's a real downpour. The rain may still be
full of radioactive materials, so we are not going to
go out until it stops.

The news seemed to perk mom up a little. She knows
that the rain my lessen the radioactive levels outside.
Since the robbery the other day, she wants to leave
the mines as soon as possible. I haven't had the heart
to tell her how ugly it is outside. Everything that wasn't
burned is rotting. The smell of death is in the air constantly. There is very little food or water. The people
all look like pictures of refugees we used to see on
the news. Everyone is frail, sick and weak. All the
children I saw were thin, with big eyes and stomachs
swollen from hunger. Mom has no idea how healthy
we look compared to the other survivors.

MARCH 25

It is still raining hard outside. It is as if the sky held
out as long as it could. Now it can't stop. The radioactivity is being washed into the river and ocean. The
ground is absorbing it too. Hopefully, when the rain
stops the radiation levels will be greatly reduced.

Dad and I went into the lower mines today to gather
food and water to trade. We also rolled two empty
fifty-five gallon metal drums into the caves and filled
them with water. We established a slug farm and two
mushroom gardens. Both of these will keep us in fresh
food for some time.

We made up two backpacks of slug meat and mushrooms. We also put together a care package of water, mushrooms, and slug meat to take to the survivors in the other mines. Dad also included some rice and a bottle of vitamin "C" tablets. Dad plans to leave the mines on the other side of the hill in the next day or so. We will drop off the care package on our way to do trading at the college. Dad says outside survivors are going to be watching and following us closely. We must leave false trails.

MARCH 27

The rain has let up. It is only sprinkling on and off. Dad and I are going to go at dawn tomorrow. All our gear is ready. We are going to suit up at the exit we regularly use, then we're going to walk through the mines to the other side of the mountain. We will drop off food and water to the cave survivors, then we will exit the mines somewhere west of here. Dad says we will follow the old road path down towards Pittsburg and then cut over to the college.

The college seems to be the only major structure that survived the nuclear holocaust—dad says because it was built almost exclusively of cement and two-thirds of it was built below ground level. The hospital that existed two blocks away is completely gone. The professors, doctors and scientists who survived recognized the fact that the college is a good center to begin the rebuilding process. They have established a medical treatment area on one level, with the Red Cross, and a communications and information center on the upper level. Usable materials and equipment have been brought to the college for use and distribution.

MARCH 29

Dad and I returned last night from a very eventful and constructive trip. We took food and water to the survivors in the western mines. They are trying to organize themselves and share what little resources they have with each other. The big man did not come out to see us. He has told the other survivors that our intervention will destroy them all. Dad told the group that we were going outside to help begin organizing other survivors. He suggested that the cave people elect a representative to go out with us the next time we go out.

Dad and I left the mines just as a bleak and gloomy morning was dawning. It took us only an hour to follow the old road to Pittsburg and reach the scorched cement walls of the college. As we approached the entrance to the former school, two young men came toward us. One was a member of the gang we had a confrontation with on our last visit. The other apparently knew my father. The young gang member's name was Frank. He was tall, thin and extremely pale. He had no hair and the gauntness of his skin made his face look like a skull. The other young man was Teddy. He had been a student of my father's several years ago. He and dad had talked on our last visit. Teddy was shorter than Frank and had probably been an athlete at some time. He had a large frame, but with little meat on it. His hair had fallen out, mostly on top. He looked like a monk.

Frank explained to dad that he and his friends had gathered many of the items on the trading list we had given him. Dad told Frank we had brought food to trade and that we may have some new needs to help other survivors we knew of. He did not explain where the other survivors were located.

Teddy told dad that he and others had gone out and contacted many survivors in the Pittsburg/Antioch area. They are arranging a meeting of any interested people, or representatives of survivor groups, to organize services and information. The meeting is to be held in five days. Dad said he and I will be there.

We went into the college and completed our trade with Frank. He was very excited about the meat. We did not explain what the source of meat was, simply calling it pork. Dad also explained the best way to prepare the mushrooms we had brought.

After our transaction with Frank and conversations with other workers at the college, dad and I started our hike home. It was raining steadily when we began. By the time we were halfway back, it was raining so hard we could barely see twenty feet ahead. Dad finally pulled off his gas mask and told me to do the same. The combination of ash turning to mud and the barren hills unable to absorb the downpour made it incredibly difficult to make it back up the hills to the mines. It was nearly dark when we finally entered the dryness of the caves. In the caves we undressed and went to bathe. We dressed and went to our caverns. Mom and the girls were waiting with warm food. I was cold, wet, hungry and tired. When I finished eating, I went in and fell asleep.

MARCH 30

I made a miserable discovery this morning. I'm waiting for dad to return so I can tell him. We may be moving out of the mines sooner than we planned. I went down in the mine to get water for mom to cook with. I was filling the water jugs when my lantern went out. I started to get out my flashlight, but I stopped. As my eyes adjusted to the darkness I saw it. The small pool of water had a slight green glow. At first I thought I had mistakenly gone to one of the contaminated pools we bathed in, but I knew that this pool was clean. It meant that the pool had gotten radioactive contamination from another source.

I took my flashlight and checked a dozen other water pools. All of them gave off a slight glow. The deeper the pools, the less the contamination. Perhaps in the deepest mines the water is still good, but the presence of poisonous gas makes it impossible to get to it.

I did not tell mom about the water. I brought water from the barrels dad and I had filled up previously.

That water is not radioactive, but it will not last long. I hope dad has a plan. We cannot survive without water.

APRIL 1

Dad and I used air tanks and gas masks to go into the lowest mines to get water. We must have over a hundred and fifty gallons of uncontaminated water for our personal use. Eventually, we'll have to drink water with radioactive contamination. Dad says the radioactivity isn't enough to kill us, but the accumulation of radioactivity in food, water and air could cause major changes in our bodies. I have cut my hair short (boyish), but I don't want it to fall out. I also don't want my teeth to fall out, like survivors outside.

APRIL 2

Dad, Nellie, Jamie, and I went to the mine entrance we had first used to enter the caves. We all helped dig out the opening and clean away the rubble. Nellie and Jamie made little rock piles in the tunnel. I collected wood and piled it in the tunnel. Dad wore a gas mask and shoveled dirt out the opening. When the opening was cleared, dad had us put on cloth filter masks that he had gotten from Frank in our trading visit. He told us anytime we are outside the mines, we are to wear a filter mask. This will reduce the amount of radioactive dust we breathe.

The girls were excited about being outside. They giggled and played just outside the entrance. It isn't raining right now, but the sky is still grey and overcast. Also, the temperature is dropping. If it rains again, it could snow. With no shelter and heat, the outside survivors would freeze to death.

Dad and I are going to the meeting at the college tomorrow. A lady named Donna is going with us. She is a nurse who lives with the other group of mine survivors. She wants to attend the meeting and talk to the Red Cross about the health of her group. We are leaving at dawn. We will wear filter masks instead of gas masks and we are taking food to trade.

APRIL 5

We just got back from the meeting. It lasted two days. Over eight hundred people showed up. Some were in remarkably good condition, even after three months exposure to radiation. Some who came were hideously scarred. Many who came looked near death——some from hunger, some from radiation, and some because they had lost the will to live.

I was very proud of my dad. He took charge of the meeting from the beginning. A small stage had been set up near the front parking lot area. A public address system, run off the school's generator system, allowed everyone to hear the speakers. The Red Cross gave a quick talk on what not to eat or drink, how to treat some of the common illnesses, and how to dispose of bodies. Dr. Bronson told the meeting about his information, regarding where bombs had fallen, what areas had been most affected, and the status of radiation in our areas. Teddy and Frank gave quick reports on situations they had encountered while traveling throughout the county.

Frank told the gathering that there were individuals and small gangs victimizing and preying on survivors. He said there had been reports of rape, theft, beatings, and murder. He wanted the crowd to be suspicious of strangers and to not go out alone at night.

Teddy talked quickly about insects——ants, spiders, roaches and beetles. He told the group that the ground insects had not only survived the war, but were changing because of it. Teddy said that throughout the county the insect population has increased incredibly. He also said that the insects are voracious. They are eating everything they can. He believes that soon we will be competing for food with the insects. He suggested that at some point we may even become food for the insects.

After Teddy finished talking, dad got on the stage and spoke into the microphone. I did not recognize the man who spoke. He seemed different. His voice was full of emotion and passion. He was like a coach or trainer, trying to coax an athlete to go on . Finish the race. Fourth down and inches to go. Answer the final bell. He used a lot of old sports cliches, but he made his point and the crowd listened.

He told everyone they could lay down and die or wait for the beetles to eat them. He said quitting would be easy, anyone can quit. Then in a soft, but purposeful voice, he told them that if we were going to survive, we would have to band together and organize. He took a piece of paper from his jacket and began reading it to the crowd. It was a list of suggestions:

1) In order to consolidate resources, everyone move their families to the college area.

2) The college area becomes a communal city, with the college acting as a resource and information distribution center.

3) A police force be set up to protect the college area and those living in it.

4) A council be elected to establish rules, laws, and survival plans.

5) Committees be established to deal with areas of concern, that is, food, water, electricity, lawbreakers, insects, etc.

When dad had finished reading his list, he called out some names and asked them to come up on the stage. It took me a moment to realize he had called my name. I went to the stage and stood by Frank and Teddy.

"These people are your first committee leaders," dad told the crowd. "Each one of these people has knowledge in an area important to us. I will tell you their assignment. If you can be of assistance to them, let me know. Form up into small groups and discuss what can be done. I will come around later and meet with each committee."

Up to this point the large crowd had seemed lethargic and inattentive. It was like dad had to waken them and give them directions. He stood in front of Teddy, with his hand on Teddy's shoulder, and told the crowd Teddy needed help in organizing an expedition up north to meet with officials there who could send food. Anyone who could help him should talk to him over by the handball courts. He went and stood by Frank. He told the crowd Frank was an expert on gangs. He would be in charge of a crime committee. Anyone interested in helping Frank should talk to him by the gymnasium wall. Dad put Dr. Bronson in charge of a committee to look for building materials to construct living quarters around the college grounds. He put Donna, the nurse, in charge of a committee to round up survivors and bring them to the college. Another man, Larry, who looked like no war had happened because he had all his hair and teeth, was assigned a committee to deal with the insects. When all the committees had been assigned, dad stood next to me.

"My daughter and I are planning a trip to the ocean to get seafood. We would appreciate any help we can get", dad said to everyone. Then he again prodded the crowd. "Okay, people; now is the time to sign up for one of these committees. Let's do that now."

The crowd stirred slowly, but it moved. Dr. Bronson stayed on the stage and continued to urge the survivors to join in and help organize. He also set up another committee. Donna was given charge of listing the names of all the survivors and helping people locate family and friends who may still be alive.

Dad and I left the stage and began conversing with the people in the crowd who just stood and stared. The ones who were lost and in shock. We told them to go to one of the groups and volunteer to help. Some moved off to participate in a group. Some just continued to stare. They were like zombies. They're in shock; more dead than alive. I wanted to grab them, shake them, slap them, scream at them, but I knew it wouldn't help.

By the end of the day, the survivors with will and the desire to live had become active and animated. The groups were meeting around campfires and discussions were long and involved. Our group consisted of twenty-two, counting dad and I. Five other women and myself, and sixteen men. Several of the men were avid fisher-men. One woman, Samantha, was trained in marine biology and knew a great deal about California's ocean life. There was also a young man named Jerry, who had been a commercial fisherman and owned a large fishing boat.

The two largest and most active groups were Dr. Bron-son's building group and Donna's survivor roundup group. There were almost two hundred people involved and they were already working together on where survivors would be housed and how soon.

I followed dad around the next morning as he met with each group. He listened to their plans, any problems and made suggestions. By noon, every committee had a plan and was acting on it. Dad suggested that two or three members of each group be appointed as repre-sentatives. The representatives would meet in the next day or so and discuss problems and progress. A meeting was set and dad and I headed home. Donna stayed behind.

APRIL 6

Dad has told mom that we will stay close to the caves until the outside survivors get more organized. He feels it is going to be awhile before the survivors really get motivated and begin establishing a new community. I know from our conversation on the way home that he is worried about some people becoming too powerful and misusing their power. He is also concerned that groups outside our area will come in and jeopardize the new community. He thinks we should remain aloof until everything around the college is more stabilized.

Dad and I are returning to the college tomorrow for the meeting with the representatives of the committees. We are also going down to the river with Jerry, the fisherman, to look at a boat he says may be salvageable.

Nellie has been bugging dad to go with us. He says she will get to go soon, but now she must stay and protect mom and the girls. She accepts that as an important role, but mom gets mad at dad. Mom says it makes Nellie impossible to manage. She walks around the cave giving orders and talking like dad.

APRIL 8

We returned from our second meeting at the college. Some good and bad things are happening. The committees are all progressing well. Teddy's group is planning on making an excursion up north in a week. They are going to try and contact the military or Red Cross and get aid for the survivors here. Our fishing group has found a forty foot fishing boat that sunk in shallow water near the dock. Water protected the boat during the nuclear fires. Jerry says we can raise it and refit it in a month's time.

At the committee representative's meeting things got a little heated. Each committee feels it is more important than the others. The housing group has been given priority over all else. All the representatives voted that preparing living quarters for the survivors is most important. Teddy's group going north for help was given second priority, but only after dad told the meeting that we'd better become dependent on ourselves and not rely on outside sources who need what they have for themselves. He also explained that good amounts of fish and shellfish could be gotten from the ocean every week.

Dad told me after the meeting that most of the representatives were well meaning, but followers, not leaders.
He said soon there will be a power struggle by stronger,
more ambitious members. They will try to gain power
and control over people and resources. They will use
their strength as leaders to control the food, or water,
or housing. He told me once someone gets a bit of
power, or control, that person will try to eliminate
any opposition, or criticism. Dad says to make contacts
among all the groups and listen closely to what is said
and done. "Knowledge is a quiet, but subtle power."
Dad confided with a wink.

Before we left to return to the mines, dad told Jerry
we would bring fresh food to trade for whatever he
needs to fix the fishing boat.

APRIL 9

Mom made her first visit outside. She was really happy
when she got out of the mine. She and I walked down
the sloping path we had used the night we had come
to the mines. We stopped on a small bluff that overlooks
the steep canyons that had once housed a mining community of several thousand people. In the far distance,
to the north, we could look between two great hills
and see a tiny portion of the Sacramento River.

After awhile mom realized that all the beautiful trees,
birds and animals that had once covered this park area
were gone. She got very quiet and sad. Shortly, she
suggested we go back inside.

On our way back up the path to the cave entrance,
I pointed out some young seedling trees that were pushing their way up through the muddy ground. Mom gave
a weak smile and said she hopes it will grow back someday.

APRIL 11

Nellie and dad went to the college yesterday. Dad took Jerry some food to use as trade items for getting building materials. He also went to see Teddy before he leaves for his trip up north. There are five men and one women going with Teddy. They are carrying letters from Dr. Bronson at the college, the Red Cross representatives, the representative committee and from dad. Teddy's group is supposed to make contact with the Red Cross and National Guard in the north. They are seeking any aid they can get for the survivors in this area. The group is carrying large, empty backpacks in hopes of returning with food and medicine.

Dad spoke briefly with Teddy about watching out for looters and getting some measuring devices from the National Guard. There is only one Gieger counter in all of Contra Costa County. Teddy told dad not to worry, that he was sure he would return with food and medicine. He believes they can set up a permanent supply line to the north.

The group is crossing the river on a raft. They are going across where the Antioch Bridge used to be. They figure it will take two full days walking to reach one of the aid stations. They expect to be back next week.

Dad does not put a lot of hope in the success of their trip. He feels that the people in the north are going to be protective of what they have.

While they were at the college, Nellie traded a pen knife, a filter mask, some wool socks and a Dr. Seuss book for a pack of Spearmint chewing gum and two jigsaw puzzles. Dad said she's a real wheeler-dealer.

APRIL 13

Dad gave me several packs of seeds he had found in the ruins of the old Handyman Store. There are radishes, carrots, tomatoes, zucchini squash, chard and string beans. He said I should try planting some in the cave and some outside. He doesn't think they'll grow at all, but it's worth a try.

I planted a huge garden in one of the large caverns. I set up two sun lamps we had traded for and hooked them to two car batteries we had dragged into the mines. There is plenty of moisture and the sandy soil is rich in minerals. I will turn the lights on for a short time each day and see if anything grows.

The rest of the seeds I planted just outside the mine entrance on a flat piece of ground. I will have to carry water outside when it doesn't rain and the water will be lightly contaminated. Considering the radioactivity of the soil, I don't think the water will matter.

I had to build a fence around the outside garden to keep out animals. I used rocks, wood and chicken wire to enclose the plot. I also put tin foil and cloth in the wire to make noise and flutter in the wind.

I don't hold out much hope for the gardens, but it gives me another project to work on and keeps me busy. I don't like just sitting and having time on my hands. I remember how I used to waste time, watching TV and gossiping on the phone, now it seems very precious. It is not to be wasted.

APRIL 14

One of the cave survivors from the western side of the mountain came by today. He startled mom and dad. They were sitting and talking and this guy just came walking in. He apologized to mom for not knocking, but he said he couldn't find a door.

The guy's name is Floyd. He came to tell dad that Donna is going to move to the college area permanently. Most of the cave survivors are going with her. The big man and some of his followers are staying in the mines.

Donna sent Floyd by with two other messages. Beware

of the big man and there will soon be living space for us near the college. Dad thanked Floyd and told him to thank Donna. He told Floyd we had some projects to complete here before we would be moving to the college.

Floyd apologized again for barging in and left. He looked like the majority of the outside survivors as he turned and limped out of the cavern. He was slight of build, under nourished, quickly balding, dirty and weak from hunger and radiation. After he was gone, mom spoke for the first time since he entered the cave. She said Floyd had been one of the two men who had robbed us. He was limping because Nellie had stuck a knife in his thigh.

Dad shook his head and said Floyd must have had a change of heart. He no longer followed the big man.

Nellie And The Mangy Raccoon

APRIL 15

Nellie and a mangy raccoon squared off today near the outside garden. The raccoon was way out of his league. He came up behind Nellie while she was helping me water the mounds of seeds. The raccoon started making weird squeals and chirping noises. Nellie didn't even hesitate. She turned and hit the raccoon sideways with the paint bucket full of water. The raccoon rolled across the ground several times, then came to a halt on its hind legs. It was facing Nellie with its front paws held up like two hands in front of it. It was hissing and growling and trying to look as ferocious as it could. Nellie got a quick run up and punted the raccoon about ten feet. This time when it stopped rolling, the raccoon just waddled away with a slight limp.

The whole scene had been comical, but something about it disturbs me. Nellie will turn nine years old in a couple of months and already she seems like an adult. It's like she skipped childhood. At eight years of age she has lived through an atomic war, learned survival techniques, experienced real violence. She doesn't talk like she's eight. Everything she says and does is business like. She has a real strength about her that is admirable, but there is also a sense of violence. I know in a given situation I could be violent, but it scares me. Nellie gives me the feeling that she would enjoy a violent confrontation. She's always been a little brat with a mean streak, but now she seems cruel, maybe even vicious.

I hope when we finally move to the college and she is around other kids her own age she will lose her violent nature. I love her, but at times, she scares me.

APRIL 16

Tomorrow dad, Nellie and I are going to the college to see if there has been any word from Teddy's group. We also want to go by and visit Jerry. We're taking him some food to trade and help him work on the boat, if he needs it.

Mom doesn't like being left behind with Jamie and Jackie, but she knows the girls can't make the trip too easily. While we're out of the mines she sits in her cave room with the girls and a shotgun. If anyone makes the mistake of entering that small cave room, they'll never know.

I'm taking along some trade items tomorrow that dad doesn't know about. I've packed a six pack of the cokes we found, a homemade sling shot, extra slug meat and a small buck knife. Frank told me he thought I might be able to trade for a birthday present for dad. Frank said he saw what I'm looking for.

APRIL 18

Two good items from yesterday's trip to the college: Jerry has made real progress on the boat. He is really a hustler. He has people doing work on the boat and bringing in materials by promising fresh fish. He tells people he has nothing to trade until he gets back from fishing. He got one guy to trade a hundred gallons of gas for fifty pounds of fish. Apparently the guy found gas tanks under the ground where a gas station had been. By some fluke, the tanks had not exploded. The man has done well by trading gas for what he needs.

Jerry got another man to trade paints and lacquers he found for fish we don't even have yet. With the materials he has accumulated and the committee members working full-time, the boat could be ready to go in another week or so. Jerry and dad talked about how and where they would go to do the fishing and diving.

The other good news from yesterday's trip was dad's birthday present. I gave Frank my trade items and he was back an hour later with the present. I had a heck of a time taking it apart and packing it so that dad didn't see it. I've got it hidden in my cave room. I can't wait for dad to see it. He's going to freak.

There was no news about Teddy and his group. Donna said she'd send word to us when Teddy returned. She and her group from the mines are keeping our hiding place a secret. Donna says we deserve that because we helped them.

APRIL 19

The sun came out briefly today. I was outside near the garden when a break in the gray sky opened up. The sun was only out for about a half hour. There was also a few patches of pale blue peeking through.

I wish it would warm up. Somehow the gloomy weather adds to the gloominess of our situation. Everything is so gray. The ground is a gray mud. The sky is a hazy gray. The rubble that was once houses and businesses is now ash gray mounds. The mood of the survivors is gray and somber. If the weather would warm up and the sun would shine, it would raise everyone's spirits. Mom would cheer up, too.

The cold weather has taken a few lives. Those survivors who have not found adequate shelter are at the mercy of the rain and cold. The temperature outside has remained below fifty degrees since the war. This time of year is usually warmer and wetter.

APRIL 21

Teddy showed up at the cave entrance today. His group returned yesterday. He came with a letter from the National Guard commander up north. It was addressed to dad.

I was checking my outside garden when I saw Teddy coming up the valley. He was wearing a stocking cap and a filter mask, but I recognized him by his camouflaged hunting jacket. We talked briefly at the garden, then we went into the mines to see dad.

I introduced Teddy to mom. She told him she was glad he had made it back safely. We all sat by the fireplace and listened to Teddy as he described his trip. Dad questioned him about damage in the north and other conditions.

Teddy said his group walked an entire day before they saw any signs of life. At first, everything looked the same as our area, then the group began seeing areas that were not burned. They saw trees and grass. They passed Vacaville and were all the way to the outskirts of Marysville before they saw a human survivor.

The old man they met showed only minimal radiation effects. He told them where the Red Cross was located and how to get there. The group went to a high school gymnasium in the center of town. The walls were lightly scorched and all the windows were boarded up. The Red Cross had collected food, blankets and clothing to distribute to the local people. Water was the one item that was extremely scarce. The Feather River had dried up after the war. Recently, the rain had begun to refill the river bed, but the water was radioactive.

The Red Cross in Marysville directed Teddy's group further north, to Chico. It took another day of walking to reach the college campus in Chico. The town was totally intact. Teddy said it was as if no war had happened. The effects of radiation are hard to detect.

The group went to the aid station set up at the Bell Memorial Union Building on the California State University campus. They asked questions, got information, told the authorities of the survivors in our area. According to Teddy, there is food, clothing, blankets and fuel in the north. The missile warheads and fire that killed and destroyed here did nothing in Chico. The bad news is the growing radiation and lack of water. The northern part of the state is accumulating a lot of fallout from further north, Washington, Oregon and even Alaska.

People who had not been affected by the fire and destruction of the first strike are now feeling the after shocks. Their plight may be the plight of all survivors who lived through the rain of missiles——slow death from the war's by-products; radiation, famine, pestilence, drought, disease and the inevitable chaos.

Teddy's group returned with some food and medicine, two Geiger counters, a map of known destroyed areas, a short-wave radio, and the knowledge that thousands of survivors in the north have just begun to feel the terrible reality of the war.

The last item Teddy discussed was the reply to dad's

letter. Dad read the three typed pages to himself before he shared the information with us. According to the responses to dad's inquiry, the government leaders of the United States are gone. The final word from the President, Vice-President and Cabinet members came from an airplane somewhere over the Atlantic Ocean. There are pockets of survivors all across America and in some foreign countries. The military is working to establish communications and supply lines to all survivor groups. It is estimated that half of the country's population is dead. Radiation, illness, and starvation are still killing people. Military law is in effect and each area is requested to support existing law enforcement, or create a police force. Top scientists are gathering in northern Texas to discuss a rebuilding program and survival plans. According to the National Guard commander in Chico, this is still the United States, we are still American citizens, and we are to act as such until a formal government is established.

Teddy left before dinner. The family has been quiet ever since. The news from the north is not as good as we had hoped, but I feel a sense of release. It is comforting to know that there are more people out there. It gives my mind something to cling to. Since the war, I have felt detached, alone. It was as if this family was stranded on a small island. Even when we went outside, nothing seemed real. Everything was dreamlike. Now I know that there are people and plants. There are authorities somewhere, making things right and making it safe. It's just a matter of time before this nightmare ends. I must hang on until it's over.

APRIL 23

There was another meeting of the committee representatives today. Dad and I came down for the meeting and to see if Jerry needed any help with the boat.

The committee meeting was a rehash of what had already been said. Teddy gave his report and reaffirmed what dad had told them previously——we have to become

self dependent. The people up north need what they
have and cannot be of much help to the survivors here.
Donna and Professor Bronson told the group that all
the survivors in our area have been contacted about
moving to the college area. Construction of living
spaces at the college has begun. The first area to be
built on is the parking lot in the rear of the school.
The building program and the survivor roundup will
continue. The fishing boat and our trip to the ocean
have now taken on new importance. The main concern
of the committee is that there are no fish left in the
ocean to catch. They feel this is possible because there
have been no fish caught in the river here. The water
level in the river is about ten to twelve feet lower than
before the war.

Sam, Samantha, the marine biologist in our group has
told us that fish and shellfish close to the shore line
may have been wiped out in the nuclear storms, but
in deeper water the sea life should be well. She is not
sure what effects will occur from all the radioactive
ash being washed into the sea.

Jerry will be making a trial run in the boat in a day
or so. He says the boat is in good condition and only
the engine is a concern. The engine is made up of parts
of a dozen different motors. Soon, we'll know if it
works.

APRIL 25

Jerry, dad and I went out on the boat today. We went
west as far as what was left of the Benicia Bridge.
The boat ran fine. The engine conked out twice, but
Jerry made some adjustments and the motor worked
well.

I remembered riding up the river in my Uncle Pat's
boat last summer. From the water, you could see the
towns, the bridges, roadways on the shore and the Navy's
moth ball fleet near Suisun. Now there is nothing. The

Benicia and Crockett Bridges are twisted lumps of melted metal sitting low in the water. The ships that were
the moth ball fleet are now huge masses of metal all
fused together, no longer distinguishable as former
ships. The river itself has changed. The water is a
muddy gray color and full of floating debris. The level
of the water is down and large ash colored sand bars
are visible all over the river.

Jerry and dad plan to make an overnight trip to the
coast in two days. The crew will consist of Jerry, Sam,
dad, Phil and myself. The rest of our committee is
going to start preparing racks for any fish we may bring
back.

The representative committee has already decided
that any seafood brought back would be turned over
to them for distribution to all survivors. Dad and Jerry
have informed the committee representatives that
a small percentage of fish goes to the boat committee
and for trade. There is a lot of growing bad feeling.

APRIL 27

I am sitting on a rock overlooking the Pacific Ocean.
It is beautiful. I estimate it to be about three or four
in the afternoon. I came ashore in a small rowboat
with Sam. She is checking shell life near the shore.
I am standing guard over her and the small boat. It
is foggy and wet here, but it looks the way it has always
looked. I'd bet that Indians sat on these same rocks
a thousand years ago and marveled at the beauty and
power of this ocean. Its constant pounding is like the
pulse beat of a great sleeping giant. You can feel its
rhythm, its flow. It is alive and its food will keep us
alive.

The trip here started at sunrise this morning. It took
us about an hour to make our way from Antioch to the
mouth of San Francisco Bay. The land from Point Richmond to Oakland is virtually flat. There is an occasional
remnant of a building, or tower, or some other structure,

standing solitary watch over devastated wasteland. The city of San Francisco is a ghostly collection of burned out building frames. Great girder skeletons now stand shakily against the ash covered hills that once housed thousands of souls. The once majestic Golden Gate Bridge is little more than blackened spires sticking out of the muddy gray waters of San Francisco Bay.

We had some difficulty getting outside the Bay because of large silt deposits that have built up at the entrance. All of the soot and mud that is washing down the rivers is accumulating in the mouth of the Bay. We cleared a sea trench near the Marin headland that was less than ten feet deep.

Once outside the Bay, we headed north along the coast in water that was calm and a deep, rich, Kelly green. It took only another hour of chugging steadily along the shore line to reach the area Jerry said would be good for fishing and diving.

We tried several areas before we started catching fish. Dad said he thinks we're close to Ft. Ross. Dad and another man, named Phil, are diving for Abalone, crabs, sea urchins and scallops. They are free diving (without breathing equipment) in fifteen to twenty feet of water.

Most of the forests along the coast burned. Just above Jenner, the fires stopped burning. There is still lush green coastal vegetation as far as Van Dam. That's the farthest point we went. There is a lack of wildlife and birds. Not even seagulls came out when we cleaned fish for dinner.

Sam is almost finished with her work in the tide pools. She says she is going to help me cut up a bag of bull kelp. She told me it is an excellent fertilizer and will help my gardens. We will be heading back to Antioch tomorrow around noon. We probably have close to a ton of fish and shellfish. That ought to impress the survivors when we get back.

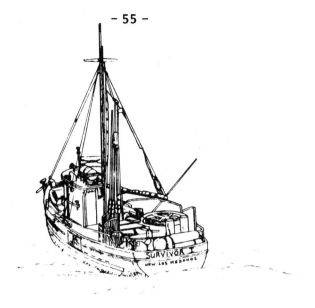

Survivor I

APRIL 28

Just a quick note from the boat (christened Survivor I). Before returning to the boat, Sam and I met an old man. His name is Jonah. He has snow white hair, sky blue eyes and a tanned, leathery complexion. He lives close to where we were fishing. Jonah told us he didn't know there had been a war until a week after, when survivors from south of him started passing his home. He is in his seventies and had been a retired Navy man. He has helped many survivors set up small farms and fishing huts and make it further north to an aid station. Jonah told us there had been some looting and vandalism, but the local residents had dealt severely with all law breakers.

The old man mentioned that there are several working generators we could get from people in the area and that he would be interested in showing us how to drill for water. He is going to meet us on our next trip up and introduce us to other survivors in the area.

APRIL 30

The fish are all drying. The representative committee is quiet, for the time being. All committee projects are progressing well, and for the first time since January, I feel like relaxing. I've done my chores, I've given the girls their school lessons for the day, and now I feel like sitting here by the outside garden and doing nothing. The sky is the same deep gray it has been since I first saw it. In the distance, towards the river, the gray sky becomes a haze and obscures the horizon. The air temperature is about forty-five degrees and there is a steady breeze blowing from the northwest. The ground is a soft, mushy gray. Around the hills and valley are splotches of green and yellow. It is moss, or mold, and plant life, trying to come back from the dead.

I am lonely. I live in a cave with four other people, I work closely with dozens of the local survivors, but I am lonely. Each day goes by quickly. I work hard. All my conversations are business. I miss talking to my friends about absolutely nothing. Silliness. Every conversation now is about life and death. I have no one I can just sit down and talk to. Dad and I talk a lot on different subjects, but he doesn't laugh and cut up anymore. He even gets a bit angry when I make silly remarks. Mom is too depressed all the time. I try to talk to her and she says she's not in the mood, or not to make light of our situation. Nellie is fun to giggle with and play games, but I can't really talk to her.

I have been wondering lately about my future. Before the war, I only had to worry about getting good grades, not talking too long on the phone and zits on my face. Now, my life revolves around finding food, surviving radiation, and protecting my family. I wonder if I'll ever have a boyfriend, or travel to other states, or count stars in a clear sky.

When I was little, I dreamed about marriage and kids and boyfriends and dances. I thought about what kind of job I might have when I grew up. I am tall and slender and I thought about being a model. I was learning to play guitar and thought about being a rock star. My favorite class in school was English and I enjoy writing. I could have been a great writer, or journalist. Now, there is no one to read even my diary.

MAY 1

Mom has been talking to dad about going with him to the college. She says she needs to get out of the caves and get away from the girls.

She is very tense and irritable lately. She has been sewing clothes for Jamie and Jackie and yells every time she's interrupted. I guess she is going stir crazy.

Dad has told mom that she can go with him on the next trip to the college. His reluctance comes out when he talks about going with her outside. She has not yet seen the real effects of the war. Dad and I, even Nellie, have become somewhat accustomed to the sights, sounds and smells of this new world. Mom may be really freaked out by what she sees outside. I guess dad has decided that she needs to see for herself. Sooner, or later, she is going to have to face life as it now is.

MAY 3

Mom and dad left this morning for a visit to the college and the fishing boat. Dad is bringing Jerry a load of mushrooms and picking up some dried fish. It will give mom time to see all of the Antioch area and outside survivors. I imagine she will be very depressed when she gets back. Dad tried to forewarn her that she might be shocked by what she sees outside, but I'm not sure she understands. Nellie and Jamie are doing reading lessons in mom's cave room. Jackie is laying in front of the fireplace staring at the fire. Jackie is a very contented baby and never seems to fuss. She is almost a year old and appears to grow bigger each day.

I took out dad's birthday present this morning, after they left, and cleaned and assembled it. His birthday is next month. He will be thirty-six. He told me once that he had done more in his short lifetime than most men do in two lifetimes. From his experience and knowledge, I'm sure he is right. His foresight saved us and keeps us alive. I wish he could relax. He is constantly doing something to improve our situation, or to help the other survivors get organized. I don't think he sleeps well at night. I often hear him rustling around in front of the cave fireplace. I know he worries about us. I'm sure he worries about mom, too. His sandy hair is starting to turn gray quickly. He is beginning to grow deep creases in his smooth face. Each day he looks more and more like his father, Grandpa Tineford. If grandpa was still alive and they stood side by side, they'd probably look like brothers.

I can only hope that tensions relax at the college and our situation becomes more stable. I'm sure dad would slow down and concentrate more on fishing and building a home for us. Maybe next month our world will not look so bleak. Perhaps dad will not be constantly on guard, or on alert, and stop trying to help everyone.

MAY 4

I was amazed when mom came in last night. She was smiling and laughing and making jokes about some of the people she met. At first, I thought she was just putting on an act for our benefit, but she is still in a good mood this morning. She told me she and Donna had a good talk about us all moving to the college area. Seeing and being around other people, even nuclear war survivors, seems to have boosted her spirits remarkably.

I asked her where she and dad went and what they did. She told me they went to the college first. She was really tired because it was her first real exercise in

over four months. She spent time with various individuals and committee members. Then, the two of
them walked down to the river to see Jerry and the
boat. Jerry and Sam were trying out some new casting
nets, so mom got to go out for a quick ride on the boat.

Today she is tired and sore from her long walk, but
she seems calm and a lot more at ease. Maybe just
getting out and away from these caves was what she
needed. Maybe it's having everything put in its proper
perspective that helped. Whatever it is, I'm glad she
is smiling again.

MAY 5

Dad picked up plans for a solar still from the college.
We spent all morning getting materials together to
build a small unit outside the caves. Dad's not sure
a solar still will work since the sun never shines. He
says he thinks whatever ultraviolet light gets through
the overcast will activate the still.

From the still we can get methanol and ethanol. These
are highly combustible alcohols and can be made from
any garbage materials. As they rot, they give off methane gas. The still will capture the gas and convert
it to a usable liquid.

Dad and Jerry have talked about converting the boat
over to run on alcohol instead of gas. The supply of
gasoline is scarce and it would be difficult to manu-
facture. Alcohol can be made from almost anything,
including human waste. Jerry has also been working
on assembling a car. He has enough pieces to assemble
a dune buggy type vehicle that would run on alcohol.
Dad says we can even make lubricants from alcohol.

It seems funny that a year before, the world was screaming about the price of oil and gas. All along, we could
have converted to alcohol fuels and eliminated the
whole problem. The country could have set up a whole
synthetic fuel industry and employed millions of people,

cleaned up the environment, and produced a cheap fuel.

Dad says the government used to pay farmers not to grow crops on parts of their land. The farmers could have produced crops that could have been turned into methanol. Dr. Bronson told dad that the people who made Volkswagons had already manufactured an engine designed to run on alcohol. He said that in Brazil, before the war, seventeen percent of all the cars ran on alcohol.

It seems ironic that there is a fuel, made for a few cents a gallon, that doesn't pollute, is an inexhaustible resource, and it took a nuclear war to make us see it.

The Girl's Pet, Hoppy

MAY 6

While I was out helping dad dig a pit for the solar still, I noticed some movement in my outside garden. I thought there was an animal eating the seeds, so I went to check. The movement turned out to be a bird! A Bluejay! It is the first bird we've seen since before the war. Even at the coast there were no birds.

The jay was hopping around the seed mounds and pecking off the scrawny little seedlings that had recently started to appear. I started to call dad over, when I noticed that the bird was deformed. His body, head and wings were disproportionate and he only had one leg. I picked up a burlap sack on the ground and gently tossed it over the bird.

As I climbed into the garden, to hold the sack down, I called dad to come help me. He came quickly and climbed into the garden with me. I told him I caught a bird and asked him to help me get it inside. He looked very skeptical, but he scooped the bag up gently and carried it into the mines. We got the bird back to our cavern and I called the girls out to see the surprise I brought them. We all gathered around the burlap sack. Dad told us not to make any sudden moves, or grab at what was inside the sack.

I gently shook out the burlap bundle and the bird dropped out onto the cave floor. The girls squealed with glee as the jay shook his little body and fluffed his deformed wings. He did not try to fly. After a few moments of cocking his head from side to side and examining his new surroundings, he started to hop, on his one leg, towards Nellie. Dad whispered for her to stand very still. The bird hopped onto her tennis shoe and began to peck at the shoestring. We all giggled. When the bird determined he couldn't eat the shoestring, he hopped off her foot and headed for mom. She was wearing a pair of big, fluffy slippers that my stepfather had given her at Christmas. The bird climbed onto the slipper and started preening the long hairy material. After a minute of stroking and manipulating the fur, the bird nestled down and started to go to sleep. At this point, we all got hysterical with laughter. Mom's eyes were watering, she laughed so hard. Dad laughed so hard his side hurt. I laughed until I had to go off into the tunnel and go to the bathroom. Mom just stood there laughing with the bird on her slipper.

After awhile, mom gently removed her slipper and sat it near the warm fireplace. The bird never flinched. He stayed in the slipper all day. That evening, we fixed dinner and Nellie and Jamie fed the bird scraps of rice and mushrooms. The bird would have eaten himself to death if dad hadn't stopped the girls.

We all went to bed with smiles on our faces.

MAY 7

The girls got up early today. They have been playing with the bird and helping dad make a cage for him. The girls lure the bird out of the slipper with food, but as soon as he eats, he hops back to his furry nest.

Dad says the bird's egg must have been exposed to a large amount of radiation. That is why he is deformed. His dwarf wings are too small for him to really fly. If he flaps his wings real hard, he can hop and fly twenty or thirty feet, but no more.

The girls have named the bird, Hoppy, and he is now the family pet. Hoppy seems quite content with his new home, especially mom's slipper.

Tomorrow, dad and I are going down to the boat. We will spend the night with Jerry and leave early the next day for the coast. We will be meeting Jonah and the coast survivors and trying out our new fishing nets.

Mom and the girls will be well entertained by Hoppy while we're gone. Mom is going to finish Hoppy's cage.

MAY 9

We returned from the coast last night. It was a good

trip. We stayed on the boat until this morning, then returned to the caves. Mom and the girls were worried because we didn't return yesterday. From the boat we unloaded a ton of fresh fish, a hundred pounds of abalone, a couple hundred pounds of crab, two brand new electrical generators and Jonah.

Jonah rode back with us to spend a week. He wanted badly to see the destruction we had told him about. He was almost in tears as we traveled across San Francisco Bay. He kept shaking his head and saying how he couldn't believe man could be so stupid. He was saying how beautiful this area had always been and how sad it made him to see it destroyed. Jonah told dad he had visited the memorial in Hiroshima, Japan, when he was in the Navy. He said he didn't believe anyone could use nuclear weapons after seeing the devastation that had happened there. "Obviously, the people who should have seen the memorial, didn't," Jonah said.

Jonah's other reasons for being here are to show us how to drill for water and to invite survivors to come live up on the coast. He has told us that there is land, food, water, and other resources there. The coast survivors feel that their area would be better suited for survival and rebuilding. Jonah is to talk with survivors here and also to the representative committee.

I am very tired from the trip. I did a lot of hiking with Jonah and some diving with dad. Dad has been napping since we got back this morning. Mom is preparing some fish we brought back. Nellie is watering the garden for me. When she is done, I'm going to take a long nap.

MAY 10

I walked to the college by myself yesterday. Dad said I could go and mom didn't put up too much of an argument. I wore pants, boots, sweater, heavy jacket and a filter mask. I also wore a stocking cap over my short hair. I carried my sawed-off shotgun concealed in my jacket and a small hunting knife in my boot. I feel relatively safe when I'm outside the caves. Most of the survivors know who I am and there hasn't been much problem from outsiders coming around here. I guess the only place survivors could come from would be up north. Since things are better up north, it wouldn't make much sense for the survivors there to come here.

At the college, I spoke with Donna and Dr. Bronson. I told them about the several kegs of nails we had found in the mines and the tools that were also there. Donna said she would send a couple of workers to the mines with a pull wagon to pick up the materials.

I guess Donna and Dr. Bronson are now romantically involved. They are constantly together and are always holding hands and hugging each other. It seems strange that two people, who before the war would never have even noticed one another, are now drawn together. I wonder if it is love, mutual respect for each other's drive and intelligence, fear, loneliness, hope. He is short, pale, pudgy, with skin that has not tightened from quick weight loss and bald. He wears heavy glasses over pale blue eyes and flashes a quick smile on small thin lips that cover a mouth with no teeth. She is his age, maybe forty-five, taller than he at five foot eight. Her hair has thinned greatly and turned white. She is pale with brown eyes and has most of her teeth. Dressed in the shabby clothes available, they look like refugees from a bad dream, but they find warmth, companionship and beauty in each other.

While at the college, I stopped in to see Teddy. He has set up the shortwave radio he brought back from the north. He stays in constant contact with a dozen different operators to the north. He tells them of our progress and projects and they keep him informed of developments there. They have formed a group that tries to contact survivors and keep them aware of important news and information regarding radiation, disease, areas to avoid and developments in reestablishing a government and a national rebuilding program. Ted has also bounced his signal off the atmosphere and picked up ham operators in other states and other countries. Ted says he has had conversations with someone in Central America who wanted to know how bad the destruction was. Apparently, some countries did not receive any missile hits at all. The man to the south said that there is only a small amount of radiation, but the weather has taken a drastic change. He told Ted that the weather had been cold and overcast since late January and that constant rains have caused severe flooding.

I told Ted I would like to come down some night and stay with him by the radio. He said I'd be welcome anytime. I told him I would ask dad for permission. Then, I left.

My last stop before returning to the mines was at the boat to see Sam. Sam is one of those rare people who do not look like nuclear war survivors. She is tall and lithe, with pale blond hair. Her skin is taut against fine large bones. Her complexion is a perpetual weathered tan offset by sky blue eyes. Even in baggy, warm clothes, she looks feminine.

Sam and I talked for about an hour while she collected dried fish from the drying racks. She says the general health of the survivors is improving because of the fish and the constant building activity. She told me she believes dad may have saved us all. His ideas and plans and constant prodding of the other survivors into activities has given us purpose and reason to live. His hard work gives others hope. Sam told me how she had lived for over a month in the basement of her house. She had moved all her food, clothes, blankets and as much water as she could carry into the basement the day the missiles came. She had been well insulated by the two feet of concrete as the firestorm engulfed the city above. She said for two days her cement basement was like a great sauna. She is sure the temperature reached two hundred degrees in her sanctuary. She did not go out of her basement until her food and water were almost gone. When she came out, she found a few survivors and shared what little she had with them.

Sam and Jerry have become close friends. The boat and the fish are a mutual interest and a focal point of their energies. It would not surprise me if they soon became involved with each other on a romantic level. Jerry is about twenty-eight and Sam says she's thirty. Jerry is a big, raw-boned guy, who, despite weight loss and radiation, looks big and strong. His skin is leathery and dark and he still has a few long strands of what was once a shocking head of bright, red hair. I hope they find some peace and comfort with each other.

I returned to the mines just before nightfall. Mom saved me some food from dinner. I sat by myself in front of the fireplace and ate. I felt very comfortable and relaxed. I still do.

MAY 11

Floyd, the man who had robbed us and been stabbed by Nellie, came by today with another man. Donna had sent them with a small pullcart to pick up the nails I had mentioned. I met Floyd and Don by the outside garden. We talked briefly about the garden and the solar still nearby. We went into the mines and I took them straight to the storage area dad and I had discovered months ago. They loaded the nails and some of the spare tools we had left there. When they finished loading the cart, we all trekked through the tunnels to our living caverns. Mom fixed Floyd and his friend some food and fresh water. They ate and drank and made small talk. Don was really impressed with our quarters. He kept commenting on how lucky we were to have so much and be in a safe place. Don looked a lot like Floyd, but was a few years younger, probably twenty. He had the same pale, lean, weak look as Floyd and most other young survivors. Don's most distinguishing characteristic was a pair of wire-rimmed glasses with only one thick lens, and it was cracked.

The two left for the college an hour after arriving. I was glad when they left. They both made me feel uneasy, especially Don. Mom mentioned the same uneasy feeling to me later. We referred jokingly to Don as "Squinty".

MAY 12

I got permission from dad to go to the college one night and listen to the shortwave radio with Ted. I'll probably go the night before our next fishing trip.

Dad and mom are going to make another trip to the college tomorrow. Mom has some items she wants to try and find and she wants to see the living quarters that are being built. I think she is getting antsy about moving out of the mines. She wants to be around other people, even nuclear war survivors.

It's funny how quickly you overlook the effects of radiation that have ravaged most survivors. The need for human companionship and simple conversation allows you to ignore burns and scars and hair loss and skin blotches. The only positive remark you can make about the appearance of the survivors is that there are no overweight people, except for perhaps, Dr. Bronson, who is a little pudgy.

Our family has come out of the holocaust in somewhat better condition than most. We have all lost weight, but not to the point of emaciation. I am tall at five foot nine inches and I'm carrying a lean hundred and seventeen pounds. I have increased in strength and agility, thanks to constant exercising and hard work. Dad has dropped from two hundred and twenty pounds to about one eighty-five. Mom has lost about thirty pounds and is now close to the hundred and thirty she was when she got married. All in all, we look very fit and healthy. We've all cut our hair short for easier upkeep and we all dress in the warmest and most comfortable clothes. Because of our long stay in the mines, we are very pale, so for the most part we look like the other survivors. The major difference is in our health. We are strong and energetic, while the rest

of the survivors are slow, weak and listless. The intro-
duction of more food and meaningful work at the college
community has helped many of the survivors to regain
some of their former energy.

MAY 17

The last five days have been very busy and rather educational, too. On the fourteenth, I walked down to the
college to spend time with Teddy. When I got there,
the whole college community was buzzing with excitement. Two major events were in the process of happening. The majority of excitement was centered around
a lady, named Ann, that Frank and his anti-gang group
had found living near Oakley in an old railroad freezer
car. Apparently, she had been living there with her
husband and a small child for some time and they were
all in relatively good health. When found and brought
to the college, it was determined that she was about
eight months pregnant. Ann went into labor earlier
this morning and is expected to deliver this area's first
baby in five months. The people were very excited
and taking bets on when the baby would be born.

The other exciting news concerned the radio. For the
past several nights Teddy had been listening to
announcements on the radio concerning a national news
broadcast from Texas. Tonight there would be some
military and science reports to all survivor groups who
could monitor the broadcast. Teddy and Dr. Bronson
had set up speakers in different locations for the people
at the college to listen.

I helped Teddy get all his equipment checked out and
in top order for the evening's broadcast. The people
in Texas were sending out a constant beep signal so
everyone listening could tune in their radios.

At eight-thirty in the evening, the beep signal stopped
and was replaced by a shrill tone signal. Thirty seconds
later, a very deep, powerful voice came on the air.

"This is a broadcast of the Emergency Broadcast System. The purpose of this broadcast is to establish communication with all American survivors of the nuclear holocaust and to share plans for the Great American Rebuilding Program." This first announcement was repeated every sixty seconds over the next ten minutes. It was followed by a different voice.

"This is Leonard Stone of the Emergency Broadcast System. I will be talking with a spokesman of the United States Army regarding law and order procedures, proper use of communication channels and rescue and resupply programs in your area. I will also speak with Dr. Lester Hagen. Dr. Hagen is spokesman for the National Science Council. He will talk about survival plans, radiation, medicine, food and scientific meetings in your area."

Mr. Stone interviewed a General William Mortland, Commander of Region V, Southwestern States. The General was obviously a good ol' southern boy with a raspy Texas drawl. He explained that the military and National Guard were spreading out across the nation, linking up, and establishing law and order. He admitted that there were gangs, dissenters, reactionaries, and militants who did not want to be controlled by the military, but they were being suppressed.

The General concluded his presentation by saying that the military had things in control and that they would keep survivors informed of all that they needed to know in weekly broadcasts. He requested that radio traffic be kept to a minimum and used only in emergency situations. He also suggested that each group of survivors avoid contacts with other groups in their areas. He used some excuse of contamination as a reason. I heard Dr. Bronson say something about a divide and conquer mentality, but I don't understand fully.

When the general had completed his talk, Mr. Stone introduced Dr. Hagen. He had a high-pitched voice and a heavy New England accent. His comments were brief. He spoke about radiation and what it was doing around the planet. He said insects are mutating and becoming aggressive carnivores. He warned that the whole planet, even where no missiles came down, has been given large doses of radiation. Everyone is affected in some way. The world's weather has been drastically altered by the massive amounts of dust and debris thrown into the atmosphere. His final comments concerned meetings for all scientists, teachers and doctors that would be held throughout the country over the next month. Dr. Hagen concluded by saying the members of the National Science Council wanted to help all survivor groups and they do not agree with some of the military's reconstruction policies.

The note of dissension between the scientists and the military was very apparent to me, and from reaction around the college, it was apparent to others. The earlier mood of hope and anticipation was quickly dulled by the broadcast. An additional damper came when the announcement of science meetings was broadcast. The nearest meeting would be in Nevada. Due to the low survival rate and high radioactivity in California, Nevada would host a large meeting for Utah, Idaho, California, New Mexico and Nevada.

Teddy and I stayed by the radio all night and listened as debates raged between various radio operators. The argument centered on who was more qualified to be in charge of a national reconstruction program: military or scientists. Most of the debates stalemated on the subject of who was more responsible for the war: scientists who made the bombs and missile warheads, or the military for using them. It was very frustrating to hear people lose sight of the real point---survival!

In the morning Teddy and I walked to the bottom level to see Ann's baby that had been born during the night. It was very agonizing for me, and I'm sure for all the survivors here, to learn that Ann's little girl had been born with defects caused by radiation. The tiny baby, named Hope, was born with no arms. When I saw her, I thought of Hoppy, and I cried.

Dad came down later that day to get the boat ready for our fishing trip. When he heard the news of the broadcast, he called a meeting of the people we most frequently deal with. At the meeting were Dr. Bronson and Donna, Teddy, Frank, Jerry and Sam and most of the boat committee, Jonah and myself. The meeting was held at the boat harbor.

Dad got up and spoke slowly to the gathering. I could tell that he was controlling a lot of emotion. He told everyone that right now, and the next few days, will determine whether or not we survive. He said there will be a struggle between the different philosophies of people here and across the country. He feels we must establish our policy now, stick to it, make it work and spread it to survivors, here and elsewhere.

Dad said he believed in two important thoughts. One, that the military is not the army that existed before the war. It is now made up of men who have little, or nothing, to lose or live for. The military, or National Guard, now offers some men an opportunity to use force, power, and aggression to get what they want. Two, a police state, run and operated like a military camp, by mostly untrained and poorly educated people, cannot rebuild a new world. It can only recreate a facsimile of the old one. We need scientists, teachers, and law makers to establish a new society.

He suggested to us that we link up as many survivor groups in northern California as we could, establish ties and develop a mutual government. He reminded all of us that there is strength in numbers and that we must remain united, resolute and disciplined. California must be a role model for the rest of the country.

The following day we made our trip to the coast. It was uneventful with the exception of a good catch of fish and sending Jonah ashore to begin organizing the coast survivors. Our trip home went quickly. Jerry has learned to navigate the river quite well.

MAY 19

I have been staying close to the mines the last couple

of days. Dad has been back and forth between the mines and the college. He and Jerry are storing up all the alcohol fuel they can. Tomorrow Jerry is going to make a long trip to the east. He is going to scout the route he and Dr. Bronson will use to drive to Nevada. He is also going to bury two caches of fuel——about 20 gallons each. He says the car, fully loaded, gets about twenty-five miles to the gallon. That gives him about a thousand mile range. With the hidden fuel he should make it to Nevada and back easily.

Teddy and Frank left for the north yesterday morning. They are going to visit Marysville, Chico, Oroville, Yuba City and Redding. They are going to talk with the national guard commander, college professors, doctors, and any other officials they can find. Their goal is to gain majority support for establishing a new state government and a united rebuilding program. Someone at the college is monitoring the radio for news from Teddy and Frank.

Mom has decided that our gardens need more attention. She and Nellie have been working all day on both the indoor and outdoor gardens. Seeds outside have germinated and are beginning to sprout. I think it's because of the kelp Sam and I brought back from the coast. In a couple more weeks we may have some vegetables. When they come in I will take some to the college and have the radioactivity in them tested.

The hills outside are turning a pale green. Grass and weeds are trying to grow out of the radioactive mud. The color is not the bright Kelly green of spring, but a sort of yellow-green. At least things are trying to grow.

MAY 21

"Death Stalks The Caves" should be the title of this entry. Three people are dead, Nellie has a broken arm and a separated shoulder, and I have a clean bullet hole in the fleshy meat of my left bicep.

Yesterday, dad was up early. He ate, loaded some materials on a small hand cart and headed for the college. Nellie, Jackie and Jamie were all outside working in the garden. I was sitting in front of the fireplace making chords on a guitar that I cut out of cardboard. I heard someone enter from the mines behind me. I turned and saw Floyd walking hesitantly into the cavern. He looked quickly around the cave then gave me a big toothless smile. I said, "hello" and asked him what he was doing here. He just stood in the middle of the room, glancing around nervously and displaying empty gums through his thin, smiling lips.

I started to rise from my place on the sandy floor when I heard voices coming down the tunnel from the entrance. I looked to the carpet that served as a door to our cave and saw five people burst in. Mom, carrying Jackie, Nellie and Jamie came into the cavern followed closely by Don, the guy we called Squinty. Mom looked terrified and the girls were all upset. Squinty had a large automatic hand gun in his fist and was waving it around crazily. He didn't seem to notice me, so I made a move to grab my sawed off shotgun leaning against the rock wall. As I turned I saw Floyd's hand flash to his pocket. He pulled out a small calibre revolver and pointed it at me. I froze.

Mom and the girls came to where I was kneeling and gathered around me. Again I asked what they were doing there. Squinty told me to shut up and went to the carpeted entrance. He pulled back the carpet and spoke into the tunnel. "It's all clear, Doc. We got'em cold."

A moment later a large man in a long dark overcoat stepped into the cavern. I recognized the big man from the other caves immediately. He walked into the cave and walked around. He nodded in appreciation as he examined our lodgings. Finally, he turned to us and spoke. He said he had been planning his revenge against our interference for a long time. Now he would kill us all and take over our quarters for his own.

I told the big man to take what he wanted, but to leave before my dad returned. He laughed and said he had everything he wanted and would kill dad when he came back. Nellie's fear, or confusion, now turned to anger and she went at the big man with her knife. She aimed for his belly, but he caught her arm in mid-stroke. He held her arm, stopped for a moment, then wrenched it back and away in one violent motion. It sounded like the snapping of a green tree branch. Nellie was unconscious when she hit the floor. I ran to where she lay and sheltered her from any more violence by the big man. He made chuckling sounds and moved off towards the small caves that serve as our sleeping quarters.

While the big man spoke to his two cronies I immobilized Nellie's arm and shoulder by using cloth strips to wrap her arm close to her body. She was becoming conscious and she was in real pain. I was afraid she was going into deep shock, so I asked the big man if I could get a blanket to keep her warm. Instead, he had Floyd usher us all into my cave room. I had mom help move Nellie as gently as we could. Once in the small sleeping area we layed Nellie on her sleeping bag and covered her with blankets. Mom sat with her back against the stone wall. She had Jackie in one arm, Jamie on her lap and was holding Nellie's good hand. She looked very scared and the girls were all wimpering. I moved away from mom and the girls and sat against the wall opposite them, on my sleeping bag. Once we had all settled down, the three men went back out into the living room cavern. We could hear the big man talking and telling the other two how he would use the mines as his command post to take control of the survivors. The sounds of breakage and our food stores being rummaged through covered the sound of me assembling dad's birthday present. Mom sat and stared as I uncoverd the large plastic bag that was buried under my sleeping bag. Once I started arming myself, I moved as quickly as I could. I didn't want to hesitate. I didn't want to think or falter. I knew exactly what I needed to do and how to go about it. I was sure that if I thought about any alternatives or consequences, I would lose my concentration and nerve.

I assembled the military M-16 rifle as quickly as any trained soldier could have. I slipped in the eighteen round clip and jammed a round into the chamber. I got to my feet and moved to the cave entrance. I took a deep breath and stepped into the passageway. The flickering light of the fireplace and of one kerosene lantern lit the main cavern. From the shadow of the passageway I could see Floyd and Squinty; but the big man was out of my view. I clicked the safety off and thumbed the switch to full automatic. I held the weapon waist high and close to my body. I had never fired an automatic weapon, but I remembered what dad had said about moving forward and firing a weapon. He had said to aim by pointing your body and moving towards your target, Floyd and Squinty were my prime targets.

I took three deliberate steps forward and fired a short burst into Floyd's back. I turned ever so slightly and fired another short burst. I hit Don in the side as he was trying to turn towards me. His stomach exploded like a ripe watermelon. I took another step and started turning to my left where I knew the big man would be. He was there. His face was a mask of disbelief. He was staring at his own two man army, lying devastated by an obviously inferior enemy. When he realized his own demise was near, he fell to his knees and started blubbering like a baby. I hesitated as I thought how someone so merciless and cruel could be such a sniveling coward and expect mercy. I thumbed the switch to semi-automatic and sent the first round into his groin. After several long agonizing moments I put a second round into his stomach. After another momentary wait I yelled an obscenity at the big man lying doubled up on the floor. My yell pierced his veil of pain and his eyes flickered open. At that moment I saw the fear and pain in his eyes. It was the same fear and pain I had seen in the eyes of my mother and sisters. "Die!" I screamed as I slammed a round through his throat. I turned away not caring if the big man was dead, or

just dying. I had a sense of relief, like I had just per-
formed a badly needed bowel movement. I had just
eliminated a little radioactive waste from the planet
and felt comfortable about it. The term "capital punishment" took on a new meaning. So did the code of
Hammurabi, "an eye for an eye, a tooth for a tooth,
and a life for a life." These men had come here threat-
ening our lives and forfeited their own. I kept hearing
the words to the theme song from the "Baretta" television show in my mind, "If you can't do the time, don't
do the crime."

I had started into the passage to the bedroom cave
when the round hit my arm. I spun a hundred and eighty
degrees in the direction the bullet seemed to push me.
I fired the last three rounds in the rifle before I
completed my turn. None of the rounds hit Floyd, but
it didn't matter. It had taken the last of his energy
to fire his pistol. He was dead. I had too much adrenalin
pumping to feel any pain. I grabbed a T-shirt from
a bin and had mom wrap the wound on my arm. After
I was taken care of I went out and collected the weapons
the men had carried.

I stayed with the girls and Nellie and mom went to
the college to fetch dad and a doctor. They were back
in a couple of hours. Mom brought dad, Donna, and
a young doctor. Dr. Frantz took care of Nellie first.
Then he examined my arm. He poured some disinfectant
on the would and bandaged my arm. I felt very weak
and a bit nauseous. He told me to rest, then come see
him in a couple of days at the college. The doctor returned to the college, but Donna stayed with us. She
spent most of her time taking care of Nellie. The arm
broke cleanly just below her elbow, but her shoulder
is in bad shape. The doctor may have to do surgery
on it.

Mom and dad removed the bodies from the caves and
cleaned up the mess left by the ordeal. Mom is still
shaky and dad is very quiet, in a scary way.

My own emotions are very mixed. I was raised with

confusing standards. On one hand I heard that killing was a sin. At the same time I heard that people had to defend themselves. Millions of people have recently died because governments disagreed about different philosophies. I killed three men defending my family. I think there's a difference between the two, but I am ill at ease trying to rationalize killing.

MAY 23

Dad and mom took all us kids to the college today. Nellie has to have an operation on her shoulder. I will be staying here with her while she recuperates. Mom is planning on moving out of the mines to the college. She refuses to stay there alone. The episode with the big man has really unsettled her. Donna took her to look at the living quarters being built.

Dr. Frantz cleaned and redressed the wound in my arm. He is very good looking. He is tall and dark. He still has a lot of wavy black hair and his eyes are so dark you can barely see his pupils. He has strong, gentle hands that gave me goose bumps when he touched my arm. He said he lost his wife during the war. They were newlyweds. He will do the surgery on Nellie's shoulder.

Jerry and Sam came by the college to see Nellie. Jerry has plotted the course that he and Dr. Bronson will be taking to get to the scientist meeting. He says above Jackson, Sonora, Jamestown and other old mining towns of the gold country, there are some small survivor groups and resources. He spoke with some survivors in Angel's Camp and told them of his trip and the plans here to form a new state government. The people there were all in favor of the plan and would assist in any way they could. Jerry told the group he would keep them informed of developments.

Jerry told dad and I that the exploding missile warheads had started uncontrollable forest fires in the Sierra Foothills. The fires stopped when they reached the heavy snow areas. Above thirty-five hundred feet the forests are still intact. Highway 88 is still driveable. Jerry says he will need snow chains to make it over the mountains.

There has been no word from Teddy and Frank. Dad is a little concerned that they have not radioed back some information. He has had the radio operator here leave coded messages with radio operators up north, but there has been no response.

MAY 25

Nellie came through her surgery without any problems. Dr. Frantz says she's the healthiest patient he has had since before the war. Her arm will be immobilized for quite awhile, but it should recover fully.

Teddy and Frank radioed in this morning. According to Teddy, there was some sort of a power struggle among two ranking national guard officers. One wanted to tighten marshal law and wait for the army to come in and take control. The other is a supporter of a self-governed California. Apparently there was a skirmish in the coastal hills between Redding and Fort Bragg. The national guard commander against a new California government was killed and his men surrendered.

Frank says there are still individuals who feel that we must wait for the Army to come into California and establish a military government. These people are very outspoken and somewhat militant. Frank's feeling is that they will make trouble, so that the rest of the survivors can't get organized.

It has been decided that an initial meeting of all survivor groups in California will be held in ten days. It will convene in Marysville, the most central location. A straw vote of survivors here shows that dad is the best person to go to the meeting and represent our area. Dad is torn. He wants to attend, but he doesn't want to leave us. I think my action against the big man has given him confidence in my ability, but not enough. Mom has told dad that as long as she can stay at the college, he can go to the meeting.

Frank and Teddy are on their way back. Dr. Bronson and Jerry are leaving tomorrow for the meeting in Nevada. Dad says he will make his decision when he has spoken to Teddy.

MAY 26

We had a big send off for Dr. Bronson and Jerry this morning. They were loaded down with fuel and food. Jerry said he'll stay under the speed limit. It was very touching watching Dr. Bronson and Donna say good-bye.

Even Nellie came out in a wheel chair to see the car drive away towards the east. Jerry and the Doc were dressed in the warmest clothes they could get. The air is cool and they are riding in an open car. When they hit the snow country, it's going to be freezing.

Dad says they will get to the meeting site several days before the meeting actually starts. This will allow Jerry and Dr. Bronson time to speak with other leaders and scientists and determine people's moods and attitudes. They are both going to quietly express the idea of a non-military government.

MAY 28

Yesterday and today have been really busy. It started yesterday when I took Nellie for a wheel chair ride through the living quarters. The spaces are made of wood and sheetrock with just the barest amount of insulation. Each cubicle is ten by twelve feet with wooden beds built against the walls. The beds are three high on each side of the space with the ladder at the end. Different styles of mattresses and bedding have been fashioned to cover the wooden bunk beds. Ducts have been built throughout the living area to carry heat from the college's boiler room. The boiler is only turned on sparingly at night. Jerry and others are working to convert the boiler system over to run off of methane gas. If it works, the system could be run constantly.

While Nellie and I toured the living area, I noticed all the young kids. I hadn't noticed that there were at least eighty boys and girls about Nellie's age. Most of the children we saw sat in their bunks and played with old or broken toys, or they sat in small groups and tried to play simple games they couldn't seem to remember.

Nellie and I were back at the college when the thought struck us simultaneously. We hurried to the learning center/library to see what materials there were. The area had been pretty well rummaged by scavengers, but we found plenty of the materials we would need. We enlisted the aid of a girl about my age. Her name was Shellie. She seemed dazed most of the time, but she would help when asked to. We gathered up paper, pens, pencils and books. We had some rulers, compasses, chalk and a portable chalkboard. The three of us lugged all the materials into the lunchroom where brunch and dinner are served each day to the survivors. We set up our materials in one corner of the room. Shellie, who had stringy brown hair and thick lips, scarred by radiation sores, said she knew where there was a ditto machine. While Nellie stayed and sorted books, Shellie and I went to the lower level of the school in search of an A.B. Dick mimeograph machine. In the back of a dark teacher's office we found the machine. We also found several reams of blank yellow paper, fluid for the machine and two boxes of ditto masters. It took two trips to move the find to the cafeteria. We would have to find a way of getting electricity to the machine, but we would worry about that later.

Once we had set up our little classroom, we all went to the living spaces and began talking to children and adults alike. We discovered that many of the children had no parents. They had adopted or been adopted, by an adult. Most of the adults and all of the children loved our idea. Starting the next day all the healthy children from five to fifteen would meet in the cafeteria for school. I would teach kids ten to fifteen and Nellie and Shellie would help kids five to nine. We decided we would teach just the necessary classes---math, reading and writing.

Today we held three hours of classes. I had twenty-seven students. Nellie and Shellie had thirty-eight. It was amazing how eagerly all the kids were to read and write. We all shared the books, paper and tables. Mostly we used the chalk and chalkboard to do lessons. This conserved our other materials.

I talked with Fred---we call him the Troll---because he lives in the college boiler room, about hooking up some electricity for the mimeograph machine. He is in charge of all the heat and electricity for the whole complex. Fred told me I could use the electrical outlet in the cafeteria in the morning when brunch is being prepared. The electricity is on in that area so food can be prepared.

In the near future, Nellie and I are going to start a newspaper. We can write up stories about what is happening here at the college and with other survivor groups. Keeping everyone informed seems somehow important.

MAY 30

Dad found out about our school and dubbed me "Jessie the Teacher." He loves our idea and says it is probably one of the most important jobs to be done. He gave Nellie and I big hugs and said keeping the young educated will insure that we don't slip back into being primitive cave men. He told me to come to the next meeting of the representatives committee and give a presentation on our school. He is going to request that the committee give our project a priority rating and make sure we don't run out of materials.

The classes are going well. Both Nellie and Shellie and I have broken our groups up into beginning, intermediate and advanced. The advanced students work at their own pace with just a minimum of supervision. The other students follow a lesson plan for each subject. All the students are very respectful and well behaved. Nellie walks around with her arm in a sling and helps the students with math, spelling and writing. When Nellie runs into a word she can't spell or a math problem she can't do, Shellie helps her out.

Most of my students are working at their own pace in math. Some are very good and some are just getting by. We all read together, taking turns reading out of the same book, then discussing what we have read. All my group can read, some better than others.

JUNE 2

Teddy and Frank returned from the north today. They have been through quite an ordeal. Survivors in the north have gone a little crazy. When the national guard began fighting among themselves, the civilians panicked. There were riots over food, clothes, water and who was going to be in charge. Frank says cooler heads have prevailed and order has been restored. Teddy says there are still many bad feelings and individuals trying to stir up trouble.

Frank and dad are going to represent our survivor group at what is being called the First California Congress. There will be approximately two hundred delegates from various survivor groups throughout Northern California and Southeastern Oregon. There will also be a troop of the national guard at the meeting to prevent any violence against the representatives.

The representative committee here has had several late night sessions to decide what dad and Frank should say at the meeting in Marysville. The biggest issue here seems to be the feeling that the northern communities that were not bombed, should share food and other resources with us. Dad says that is a ridiculous demand and feels we can become self sufficient. I'm sure dad will represent his own ideas at the Congress.

In between all their arguing, the representative committee found time to legitimize our school. All books, paper, pens, and pencils are to be turned over to us immediately. Of course, this is only until a real teacher can be found to take over the running of the school. In the meantime, Nellie, Shellie and I will continue to share the knowledge we have with other kids and call it school.

Mom has taken up residence in one of the living quarters. She and I have brought down items from the mines to make our cubicle more comfortable. Nellie, Jamie and Jackie stay with her in the cubicle. Shellie has sort of adopted me as a mother. She follows me around whenever we are not teaching classes. I have been spending my evenings by the radio, listening to the stories and mini-dramas that unfold every night. Shellie sits with me, too. She hardly ever speaks, but she listens, and some-times tears roll down her puffy cheeks.

JUNE 4

It suddenly seems very lonely here and I feel vulnerable. Jerry and Dr. Bronson have gone to Nevada. Sam and the boat crew have gone fishing at the coast. Dad and Frank left this morning for Marysville, and mom is all wrapped up in getting living quarters together for her and the girls. Teddy is the only one left who I feel com-fortable being around, but he is completely involved in the radio.

The radio is our one link to the outside world. Occasionally one of the survivors here travels away and returns, or a member of a survivor group somewhere else stops by, but the news they carry is usually days old. The radio is as close to instant as we get. Sometimes the chatter we hear is the news. We have heard cries for help, doctors giving directions on how to deliver babies, people talking while they die, and one instance where a Justice of the Peace in Oregon married a man and woman somewhere in the high Sierras. A bunch of us here stood quietly around the radio while the ceremony went on and cheered when it ended. We also radioed our congratulations from New

Los Medanos. That is the name our small survivor community has taken.

I am hoping (I'm sure everyone here is hoping) that all the survivors in California can unite together to form a new state. I think the country is in deep trouble if we don't. I remember something from school that Abraham Lincoln is supposed to have said, "United we stand, divided we fall." He said that over a hundred years ago, but it couldn't be any truer than right now. I also remember that robot of Mr. Lincoln at Disneyland. It said something about this country would never be conquered by an outside enemy. It could only be conquered from within. "A house divided against itself cannot stand," I think was the quote. It is still true. If we do not unite and organize, we will have truly lost the war.

We have no priest here. As far as I know, there is no religious leader among our survivor group. I have seen a few men and women with prayer beads and Bibles, but there have been no sermons or meetings. I wonder if any of these people are praying that the state, or country, reunites and rebuilds. I wonder how many people still believe in God. I remember when the Jehovah Witnesses used to come by our house. When dad was still living with us he would invite them in. He used to love to argue with them. I can still hear them ranting about Armaggedon. I wonder if the war was it, or if we still have that to look forward to. Somehow I think Armaggedon would be a bit anticlimactic.

JUNE 6

We got our first report back from dad and Frank this morning. Teddy rushed up from the radio and interrupted school to get Nellie and I. The three of us ran down to the radio and listened as dad gave a very short, tight report. It lasted about three minutes and sounded very cryptic. It ended with "Love to all my girls, also Sally."

I turned to Nellie to ask who Sally was, but I could tell from her expression that she was as puzzled as I was.

Teddy gave us both a sideways glance and laughed. "It's a code. Your dad and I worked out a code before he left. Wait a minute and I'll show you."

Teddy took a clipboard from the table and did some quick writing. After a moment he turned back to us. He explained to us that the first word in each sentence was the key word. The whole three minute talk condensed down to, "Meeting starts in three days. Heavy security. Many friends. All secure."

Teddy said he and dad had worked out three endings. "Also Sally," means all secure. "Thank Carol Hein," means trouble, coming home. "Tell Carol nobody home," means trouble, come need help. Apparently dad, Frank and Ted have armed Frank's police group and set up a rescue squad in the event something goes wrong in Marysville. So far everything is going well.

Teddy told us he is going to try contacting the scientist meeting in Nevada tomorrow night. He wants to get in touch with Dr. Bronson and Jerry and pass information between the two meetings.

JUNE 8

Not a good day today. It started snowing during the night. It snowed till about noon. There's about three inches on the ground. The temperature is about the mid-twenties. The heating system has been left on, but it will have to be turned off soon. If the temperature drops too much, we could be in trouble.

The kids in school wanted to go out and play in the snow, but I explained about proper clothing and frostbite. The kids were content to stand under a balcony and watch the snow fall.

When the snow stopped, we went out and cleared the roof of the living quarters so they wouldn't collapse and the melting snow wouldn't leak inside. Some of the snow was tested to see what the radioactivity in it was. Teddy said it was less contaminated than previous rain and any ground water. Some holding tanks are being filled with the snow for future water needs.

Sam tramped up from the boat this afternoon and said she would cancel this week's fishing trip if the weather does not improve. She told Teddy that there is ice forming along the river banks. If it were to continue, the river could ice up and become impassable for the boat. That would end our fishing trips permanently. The fish have become the mainstay of our diets.

JUNE 9

Today is Nellie's birthday. Nature gave her a nice present. The overcast sky broke up and for a brief moment we got to see some blue sky and a pale sun. Hard to believe it is almost summer. The sudden rise in air temperature turned snow into slush. The melting snow combines with the ash gray soil and makes a miserable mush mud that tracks everywhere.

We had a party at school for Nellie. Mom created a small cake out of food stores from the mines. She also gave Nellie a blue scarf she had knitted for her. Some of the kids at school gave Nellie drawings they had done and wrote "Happy Birthday to Teacher Nellie" on them. Nellie was embarrassed, proud, happy and a bit sad. Her eyes misted over several times during the party. She let down her little soldier defense long enough to thank everyone and tell some of the smaller kids about her last year's birthday party. As I listened, I realized how much she has been holding in her feelings, how much she misses her room, her toys, her friends. Her losses, to her, are just as important as mine are to me, or anyone else's are to them. Importance, or value, like beauty, is in the mind of the beholder. I see Nellie now not as a kid, or a little sister, but as a neat little person.

This evening Nellie got a special present. Dad called her on the radio. His conversation was open and free, not stilted the way it had been before. He told Nellie he was very sorry he couldn't be with her, but he said he had a nice surprise for her when he returned. He closed his radio message with, "Love you all and Sally."

JUNE 11

There is a small group of survivors here who have gotten themselves together and are planning to move up to the north coast. There are four men and two women. One of the women has a son about Nellie's age. The boy's name is Jason. He has been a good student at school and has become a good friend of Nellie's. She is really upset about him leaving.

The small group includes a carpenter, a heavy equipment operator and a farmer. They all want to go up north and try farming. They're going to form a small commune with the help of Jonah and other coast survivors.

Money no longer has value, but the barter system is thriving. Everyone trades what they have for what they need. People are quick to loan and share with other survivors. The gravity of our situation and our common survival instinct have brought out the best qualities in most people. There are individuals who exemplify the dark side of man. They have always existed and made life miserable for others. They are not bad enough to kill or exorcise from the community, but they are little more than parasites. They take, but never give. I suppose even a survivor society must deal with the weak individuals who are so wrapped up in themselves that they cannot give and share.

The small group going north wants to get away from the destruction in our area and they want to raise food they can trade. They are going to go up on the boat during the next fishing trip. I told Nellie we'd go up and visit Jason when he and his mom are all moved in.

I'm sorry to see good people, with valuable skills, leave this area. We need them here.

JUNE 12

I walked up to the mines today after school. I wanted to check the damage to my garden caused by the snow. Walking was difficult because the ground is so messy. Small seedling trees and grass are growing in great abundance, but not enough to hold the ground together. The dirt is constantly sliding and shifting.

My outside garden got snow on it, but the snow didn't last long enough to do real damage. Some of the leaves look frost bitten, but the quickly melting snow just gave everything a good watering. The cavern garden isn't growing much at all. Some of the seeds have broken ground, but not many and the ones that are trying to grow, look weak.

I sat for awhile near the outside garden and listened to the wind blowing through the barren hills. Two things struck me——the incredible silence and the extreme feeling of loneliness. Not lonely, like I had nothing to do, or no one to talk to. It was the loneliness of insignificance. The sensation of being a speck of sand on an endless beach. I don't feel like a member of humanity. I sit on this scorched planet with sick and dying people, but I do not feel a part of the brotherhood of man. I feel detached, disconnected, small and insignificant. A year ago I sat in Mrs. Sensmiers English class and talked about doing something important with my life, about being someone, about helping other people, and leaving a mark, a name, a legacy. Now I have no direction, no purpose. I have a complete feeling of helplessness with no control in my destiny. Everything that I say and do now seems but a drop of water in an ocean. It seems meaningless and unimportant. It would be so easy to give up, to just quit.

I returned to the college community late. I was still feeling down and discouraged, but during my walk home I had resolved that I would not quit. No matter how insignificant my existence is going to be, I'm going to live and grow and share. Maybe the only people I'll ever influence, or help, will be my family, but I refuse to lay down and die.

JUNE 15

Frank received a radio message today from Jerry and Dr. Bronson. They arrived safely in Nevada. They said there are several hundred people from all over California, Utah, Oregon and Washington, attending the meeting. Jerry said in the message that he and his alcohol car are a real hit with the scientists. Dr. Bronson said there is a great deal of arguing between the scientists and between scientists and military people. The majority of people attending the meeting are in favor of reestablishing a new democratic government. Only a small group is pushing for military leadership. However, those in favor of a military government are very vocal and organized. He insists that if California sets an example by setting up the first nonmilitary government, it will establish a role model for the rest of the country. Dr. Bronson asked Frank to relay this and other information to dad in Marysville.

Jerry concluded the broadcast by saying that they would be starting home early next week.

JUNE 17

Hoppy finds a friend. A boy about my age, who comes by the school occasionally, brought Nellie a neat surprise today. Freddy showed up when we were dismissing students and handed Nellie a shoe box. Nellie peeked inside and got really excited. She reached carefully into her box and gently removed another bird. This bird too, is deformed. She placed the black and white creature next to Hoppy and closed the cage. The two birds stood face to face and stared intently at one another. Both kept cocking their little heads from side to side. After a few moments of inspection the two birds began hopping around the cage. It looked like Hoppy was showing the new bird his new home. They sat on a perch near the water container and chirped softly to one another. Nellie named the new bird Puffy. It's deformed body appeared squat and made him look all puffed up.

The two birds are the only known pets for miles around.

They are probably the most spoiled. Hoppy has gotten constant attention since coming to New Los Medanos.

JUNE 19

It is late evening. I am sitting in the room by the radio. We returned from a quick fishing trip a couple of hours ago. Sam is in an emergency meeting with the Representatives Committee.

We reached the coast early this morning. While Sam and the rest of the crew began fishing, I took the small boat ashore to see Jonah. I trekked the mile or so from the beach to Jonah's house in about twenty minutes. All I found were the smoldering remains of the once beautiful home. I searched all around for Jonah, but he was not to be found.

I headed towards the little store and cabins at Stewart's Point. I was sure the fire had been accidental. The house had been eighty years old, it probably just caught fire and burned before Jonah could get help. My only concern at this point was Jonah's safety.

The old coast highway leads from Jonah's house to the store at Stewart's Point, but it is a lot of twists and turns. It is easier to cut across the fields and hills. I reached the last rise overlooking the highway as it passes in front of the store. I stopped walking and strained my eyes to see what all the commotion was. I was two or three hundred yards from the store parking area and standing in a thicket of scraggly Cypress trees. In green jacket and trousers I would be hard to spot.

In one corner of the parking area I could see about thirty people huddled together. In the middle of the highway was a battered black and white police van. It was blocking the road and had a blue and red light bar flashing away on top. Moving around the parking lot area were four or five men armed with what appeared to be automatic weapons.

I remained in the trees and observed the situation around

the store for about a half hour. It appeared that a para-
military group had taken over the store and were holding
all the local citizens hostage. While I watched I saw a
second battered police van pull up in front of the store.
Four more armed men exited the vehicle. From the rear
of the van they escorted two men, a woman, and a child.
The four civilians were led to where the other locals were
being held and put inside the wire enclosure that had been
hastily set up. When I decided I had seen enough, I headed
back across the hills and fields to the boat. I walked quickly and kept a watchful eye for any of the armed men.
In places where I could be seen from the highway I ran
to the cover of trees or rocks. I was glad I had brought
the sawed off shotgun, but it would be useless against
machine guns.

I reached the small row boat in record time. With fear
and worry pumping adrenalin through me I had no trouble
pushing the small boat into the water and rowing out of
the cove. As I rounded the southern point I stopped rowing.
The fishing boat that should have been there was not in
sight. I looked north thinking perhaps they moved to a-
nother fishing spot, but I could not see any boat.

There was another cove to the south that was out of my
line of sight, so I began rowing for it. Rowing with the
wind made it easy going, but my shoulders were burning
from the strain. I tried not to think about the growing
ache as I got into a steady rhythm with the oars. After
ten minutes of hard rowing I rounded the rocks that ob-
scured my view of the next cove. I felt instant relief
as I saw the fishing boat come into view. In the next
instant my heart sank. On the cliff above the cove I could
see one of the battered police vans. On the rocky beach
I could see two men standing at the water's edge. The
fishing boat had chugged to within fifty yards of the shore.
It appeared that there was conversation between the boat
and the two men on the beach.

I was a hundred yards from the boat. I stopped rowing
and stood up in the row boat. I began to raise my arms
and wave them and started screaming at the top of my
voice. I yelled for help and that I was sinking. At first

no one noticed. Then, the men on the beach started pointing. Soon I heard the boat's idling engines roar to life
and saw the white froth of her bow wake. I continued
to wave my arms and act scared. I was afraid the men
on the shore would start shooting if they knew we were
trying to make a get away.

The boat was beside me in minutes. Sam was leaning
over the rail as the boat slowed to pick me up. She asked
what my problem was. I told her to help me aboard quickly. She helped me up the small ladder and the crew pulled
the small boat aboard and secured it to the fan tail. As
I reached the deck I gave Sam a big hug and made a production of my rescue. On the cliff above the shore I could
see two men. One was observing us with binoculars. I
leaned close to Sam and told her to listen very carefully.
"The men on shore are military, or terrorist. They've
killed Jonah and are holding survivors captive at Stewart's
Point."

Sam looked at me rather incredulously then went to the
fly deck and took the ship's wheel. She made a wide turn,
first out to sea, then back towards shore. We were just
over two hundred yards from the beach when Sam told
everyone to take cover. She gunned the engines and steer-
ed south. We cleared the southern rocks of the cove before
the men on the beach could react. We came directly
back to New Los Medanos to make our report.

Sam has been meeting with the Representatives Committee
for over two hours. I have told Frank to make contact
with dad and Teddy, and explain the situation at the coast
as soon as possible. Frank has left a message for dad
to contact us immediately, but it's been over an hour.

JUNE 20

It is about four thirty in the morning. Sam came in and
was talking loudly to Frank. Her voice woke me from
a restless sleep. As I tuned into what she was saying I
rubbed the growling soreness in my shoulders. The dull
aching was a reminder of my rowing sprint at the coast

yesterday.

Sam was venting a great deal of frustration about the Representatives Committee. Her meeting to organize help for the coast survivors had been a fiasco. None of the Committee members want to commit our resources or risk our people to assist the people at Stewart's Point. Sam had argued in vain for over six hours. Without people like dad, Teddy, Dr. Bronson and Jerry to support her, the rest of the Committee members were noncommittal.

It was two hours later before dad finally returned our radio messages. His voice sounded tired and strained when he first came on the radio. He said he had been up all night trying to draft a resolution he was going to present today. He says he feels the whole California Congress may be a waste of time. He told us the entire meeting may be falling apart due to a lack of aim and cohesiveness. He thinks nothing is going to be accomplished if the delegates continue to argue and dwell on petty differences.

We listened patiently as he gave us his information. Finally, Sam interrupted his monologue. She gave a long, slow explanation of the situation at the coast and the indifference of the Representatives Committee.

There was a considerable pause when Sam finished telling dad about the situation at the coast. Frank took the microphone and checked the connection, the pause was so long. Dad confirmed he was still there and said he was sending for some people. We sat quietly for several minutes and listened to the crackle of static on the radio.

When dad's voice came on the radio again it sounded different. It was sharp, clear and excited. He asked Sam to explain the situation at the coast again, so that some of the delegates could hear the story. Sam retold the entire episode and added that the Committee here did not want to help out.

When Sam had finished dad asked her and I some questions. After an hour of radio conversation, dad gave Sam the following directions: arm twenty-five volunteers. Load the group on the boat and travel to the fishing area near Fort Ross. Wait there until signaled by Teddy.

The twenty volunteers came from the Fishing Boat Committee and the volunteer police force. We were armed with small pistols, several shotguns, several hunting rifles, and two fully automatic assault rifles. We finally left for the coast about noon. The boat was overloaded, but made good time.

At sundown Sam and Jerry went ashore for a prearranged meeting with Teddy and a small group of National Guard soldiers.

JUNE 21

At four o'clock this morning we landed twenty volunteers just south of Stewart's Point. The volunteers joined ranks with twenty-five, well equipped soldiers. The group moved to position two hundred yards south of the Stewart's Point Store. At the first light of dawn several bursts of small arms fire and grenade blasts were heard near the store. The group I was with moved quickly through the open fields to take up positions near the store and along the road. Our orders were to fire on any person, or vehicle, that came down the road.

The whole assault lasted five minutes. Dad and several soldiers had snuck into the compound under darkness. At sunrise our people moved in from north and south of the area. None of the assault group, or the hostages were hurt. Five of the terrorists died.

In all, there had been eighteen men and four battered police vans holding the hostages at Stewart's Point. A National Guard officer interrogated the captured terrorists. The terrorists said they had come out of the California desert. They had found their weapons in Barstow and picked up their vans near Los Angeles. They said that there are a few survivors living like animals in the rubble of L.A., but ninty-eight percent of the population has died. The terrorists had come north because they had heard rumors of survivors and unaffected areas. They didn't believe anyone would oppose a well armed and organized group. They claimed that they were only planning to establish an organized community and that they would be the law. None of the coast survivors had been hurt or killed. Jonah had resisted the terrorists and was locked in a root cellar during the five day ordeal.

Dad and the National Guard took the terrorists back to Marysville. Sam and I loaded our group back on the boat and returned to New Los Medanos. Dad plans on parading the remaining terrorists before the representatives in Marysville. He is going to use the incident at Stewart's Point to support the argument for a unified California—a California that cannot be terrorized, coerced, or compromised.

JUNE 24

Today is dad's birthday. Mom, Nellie and I called him on the radio. He was in good spirits. He had been in contact with Dr. Bronson earlier in the day. Dr. Bronson and Jerry are going to drive to Marysville in the next couple of days and give a report to the leaders. Dad says the incident at Stewart's Point has swung majority opinion behind establishing an independent California government.

Dad says that he and Teddy may be home in a week or so. He feels that once the representatives establish a state government, it will be self perpetuating. Elections can be held, laws established, and the true rebuilding process can begin.

Dad says he is going to recommend that Teddy be elected as representative to the State Assembly. I'm sure Teddy will be a good representative, but it means he will be away from New Los Medanos a lot. He is one of the few people I feel comfortable around and enjoy talking with. He treats me as an adult, like an equal. He never talks down to me or ignores me.

It will be good to have everyone coming back at the same time. I'm going to talk to Sam and mom about having some kind of welcome home party. Maybe we can have it on the Fourth of July and celebrate our new independence.

JUNE 29

Dad and Teddy are due home day after tomorrow. Mom, Sam, Donna and I are preparing a great homecoming party. Dr. Bronson and Jerry are in Marysville now, and the four of them are driving here together.

Everyone at New Los Medanos is invited to attend the celebration. There will be huge pots of mushroom soup, loaves of homemade bread, and barbecued fish.

Nellie and Shellie took the students out and decorated the burnt walls of the college and the asphalt parking area. They took cans of leftover paint and tossed it everywhere. There are giant color blotches all around New Los Medanos. It looks like a giant flower garden amid all the grey surroundings. The whole area looks like it was decorated by three clowns and a drunk, but it is very festive.

I am going to the mines tomorrow to see if there are any vegetables I can pick and contribute to the celebration meal.

JUNE 30

It is the evening before our welcome home/new government celebration. I am nervous and excited. I am anxious to see dad and Ted, Dr. Bronson and Jerry, and to see people being happy and smiling. People hardly ever smile. No one laughs out loud. Everyone here seems introverted and detached. We all work together, live together, have the same worries and concerns, but we don't really communicate. We don't joke or smile. I hope the gathering and food tomorrow will give everyone cause to smile, maybe even laugh.

I went up to the mines earlier today and picked a bag of weak runty vegetables. There were some squash, a few beans, a lot of squat little carrots, a dozen respectable radishes, a hybrid looking bunch of green onions that are a yellow color, but big, and several tomatoes of varying size, shape and ripeness. I had hoped there would be enough for a giant salad, but there was not enough for everyone to enjoy. Instead I had mom create a nice vegetable soup as an alternative to our common mushroom dish.

Some ladies around the complex got together and created a batch of cookies for all the kids. There is one older woman, everyone calls her Moms, who tries to organize the mothers and other women who are constantly sitting around with nothing to do. It had been her idea to do something for the kids.

Frank surprised me today. He is usually a very quiet individual. He stays close to the radio and away from most everyone. I'm pretty sure he drinks a lot. I think he has a still set up some place and makes his own alcohol. He is always trading, bartering, and dealing for things he needs. He is very skilled at making things out of junk. This afternoon I went by the radio to see if there had been any word from dad. Frank was happier and more talkative than usual. After five minutes of small talk about the radio, Frank asked if I wanted to know a secret. I told him I did and he showed me a box that was sitting in the corner, covered with a tarp. In the box were several dozen brightly covered tubes, cones, and small boxes. Frank explained that he had been collecting materials and assembling fireworks for over a month. He told me it had been his plan all along to shoot off fireworks on July 4th. The celebration tomorrow was an even better reason. Frank and another survivor named Emil are going to put on a fireworks display just after sunset tomorrow. It will be out and away from the college and living area.

There isn't much chance of fire, since there is nothing left to burn.

I am going to bed now and try to get some sleep. I feel the same type of anticipation I used to feel on Christmas eve.

JULY 2

Yesterday was one of the best days I've ever had. I think that even if there had been no war, it would have rated in my top ten.

Dad, Teddy, Jerry, and Dr. Bronson reached New Los Medanos at around nine in the morning. As if on cue, the cloud covering above parted and presented us with a hazy, but bright day. It seemed like the sun brought out the entire population to greet dad and the gang.

Everything went perfectly. There was plenty of food and everyone ate till they felt stuffed. People brought out musical instruments, pots and pans, empty bottles, and an assortment of noise makers. The impromptu band made up its own tunes and many of us danced and formed human chains, or snakes, and weaved through the crowd, hopping and kicking in time with the music.

When evening came, everyone sat on the asphalt parking lot and watched Frank and Emil's fireworks display. They set off sparklers, pinwheel , cones of sparks, small rockets that burst in the air, and a fireworks sign that said, FREE-DOM. Everyone clapped and yelled at each pinwheel and they oohed and aahed for each bursting rocket. When the Freedom sign lit up, everyone got quiet. There was a soft murmuring from the people. Then, everyone started clapping. Somewhere in the crowd people started singing America The Beautiful. Instantly the crowd took up the song. The chorus of over eight hundred voices brought goose bumps to my skin. When the final verse of the song ended, voices in the crowd started singing the Battle Hymn of the Republic. As the hymn was fading the crowd made a valiant effort to sing the national anthem.

The celebration ended shortly after the singing. Everyone walked slowly back to the living area. They carried the blankets and cushions they had brought to keep themselves warm and comfortable during the fireworks. The people were talking and smiling. Some were crying softly. People comforted each other, held hands, or put an arm across someone's shoulder. It was the perfect conclusion to the perfect day. It had been all that I had hoped for, and more.

Ever since we moved to the college area, people have been quiet, reserved, even somber. It was as if everyone thought it would be irreverent to smile or laugh. I don't know if it was a sense of guilt for being alive or if they felt a laugh would bring about a catastrophe, retribution, punishment, pain, or an end to their survival. It was as if everyone was holding his or her breath, waiting for another bomb, or their punishment. Punishment that millions of others had already received.

Yesterday ended seven months of mourning by the survivors at New Los Medanos. A weight has been lifted from the spiritual shoulders of this community. The folks here have relaxed and accepted the role of survivors, without guilt or remorse.

JULY 5

It's been three days since the celebration. I have watched carefully to see if the mood of that day would continue. I half expected everyone to revert back to their quiet, somber moods, but I have been surprisingly rewarded. Almost everyone I see, or talk with, has retained the positive feelings created by the festivities of the other night.

Last night there was a representatives meeting held so that dad and Teddy could talk about the new government, and so Dr. Bronson and Jerry could relay information from the scientific meeting in Nevada. In the past, these meetings have drawn three or four spectators, and the original seven representatives. Last night there were fifty vocal spectators who came to listen, ask questions, and offer opinions. I think any representatives who are slackers, or thought they could gain some personal advantage from their position, now know people are concerned and are watching their appointed officials.

It feels more like a community around here and I like the feeling. It is like someone put our common needs and goals into perspective. Our objective is in focus and we are looking at it together. Rebuilding our lives, our homes, and our world will be much easier.

JULY 6

It has been announced that a community election will take place August 1. We will elect a mayor, four councilmen, or women, and an area representative to the new state legislature.

Dad is going to run a ticket of people that he feels will work best together and have similar ideas and ways of working. Dad is campaigning for Teddy as our area representative, Donna as mayor, and Frank with two other gentlemen as councilmen. Frank is a local hero because of the fireworks, and Donna knows everybody by their first name because of her work as a nurse and getting relatives and families back together. Dad says he doesn't think any groups, or individuals, can muster that kind of popularity.

A lot of people have said dad should be mayor, or area representative. Many people have come by our living quarters and tried to convince dad that he should run. Dad just smiles and says he has done all he can. Now he just wants to fish, help build the community, and be close to his kids.

JULY 8

Sam and I went north on the fishing boat. While Jerry and the crew hauled in a good supply of fish, Sam and

I attended the election celebration for the coast communities at Anchor Bay. Jonah was elected area representative. He is leaving for Marysville as soon as the new council for the north coast survivors is sworn in and working.

Sam and I were given special attention at the celebration, when it was announced that we were the ones who had brought help against the terrorists. We ate fried chicken, lamb stew, and baked fish. We also got two cases of wine from the Napa Valley. Prewar wine, of course. There had been extensive damage around Napa and Sonoma, but not to the wine cellars below ground.

JULY 10

Nellie had her cast removed today. Dr. Franz put her arm in a sling and has set up an exercise therapy program for her. He says in a couple of weeks her arm will be as good as ever. The arm will heal, but I wonder what mental scars will remain.

Since there has been no summer weather, the school has continued to function everyday. The only day we haven't had classes was the day of the celebration. School, for the kids, is fun. They prefer being in class to sitting around the living area, or doing menial jobs around the community.

I remember when I was in school. I did pretty well, but I didn't really try. Most of the people I went to school with didn't really try. School was more of a duty than a privilege. Now the young kids really appreciate the chance to learn and get away from the everyday monotony of their existence. All of these students will be good readers and writers, and will be able to do basic math. Even the slowest students are avid learners. The small numbers, the individualized attention, and simple desire, make it easy for the students to learn.

Shellie, who had been little more than a zombie, is now very independent. She is still shy and quiet, but she works independently teaching students, and she works on tasks of her own choice. Occasionally she smiles and will sit and talk for short periods of time. I'm sure she spends most of her time in the evenings sitting by the radio with Frank and Emil. She feels comfortable around Frank and I think he has gotten her to talk, more than anything else.

JULY 12

This morning I went to ask Dr. Bronson if he would come and teach some basic chemistry to the older students at the school. He was delighted by my invitation and said he was sure that he had a lot of old pamphlets stored in his old classroom that we could use.

He and I went down to where the physical science classes used to be taught. Most of the materials and furnishings of the college have been scavenged off for use elsewhere. Most wooden items had been used for firewood soon after the war. Inside an overturned table cabinet we found several dozen science booklets. They were very simple, twenty-five page, cartoon illustrated, single subject booklets. One was about water, another about soil, and still another was about time. They seemed a bit simple, even to me. Dr. Bronson explained that he used the booklets for remedial science classes. He said the booklets would be excellent for our classes.

While we rummaged through the old science rooms looking for additional teaching aids, I was asking Dr. Bronson about Nevada and the people at the Science Conference. He told me that somehow Las Vegas had been missed in the nuclear holocaust. Several missile warheads had fallen in the desert, but no major towns had been hit. So much for the idea of God destroying Sin City. The modern Sodom and Gamorrah had been spared destruction while the righteous citizens of Salt Lake City had been totally annihilated. In my mind it seemed like something I should be examining closely, but I wasn't sure why.

Dr. Bronson said the majority of the people at the conference were not hideous fallout victims. He explained that a lot of people had not been directly affected by the war, and many who were had adopted ways of covering up. Some wore wigs, makeup, gloves and dark glasses. Others wore uniform style clothing that included, hats, gloves, boots, ascots, and baggy khaki jackets and trousers. He said that there were almost a thousand representatives to the conference. They were wandering the brightly lit streets that were packed with refugees from other areas that had been devastated.

According to what the scientists were told, less than a hundred million American are alive in America today. Another ten million are expected to die by the end of this year due to the direct effects of nuclear fallout and diseases associated with it. Another two or three million are going to die from hunger, weather, and epidemics.

The scientific community thinks the weather is going to get colder and remain bad for several years. Depending on the severity of the weather and how well people are adjusting to it, the number of deaths could increase.

On a brighter note, there are some major industrial areas that are still capable of producing needed materials. Some of these areas have gone into mass production of blankets, bedding, and warm clothing. Still other areas are pumping out medicines, synthetic fuels, water purifying units, and synthetic food supplements. The military and scientists are working to get the materials and supplies out to the people as fast as possible. Communication centers have been established everywhere and more and more people are being contacted and informed everyday.

Dr. Bronson says we are lucky. We have a central location and are ahead of a lot of areas in the rebuilding process. California will have the first organized area government and the first postwar city built in this country—New Los Medanos.

I left Dr. Bronson next to the entrance of the living quarters he shares with Donna. I thanked him for his time and help and told him I'd see him in class in two days.

JULY 18

For four nights we sat by the radio and listened to a great drama played out by faceless voices. The voice of Death and Doom spoke in a clipped English accent. The voice of Hope was young, hopeful and energetic. In the end, Hope prevailed because Death and Doom had not calculated all the variables.

Late in the evening of July 13, Frank picked up an extremely strong distress signal coming from a great distance. Frank, and many other radio operators triangulated the signal and determined it was coming from somewhere in Colorado. After nearly twelve hours of trying to make contact with the distress signal source, the signal went silent. Minutes after the signal terminated, and with every operator in America listening, a voice came on the airways. It was the voice of Death and Doom. It was a Lieutenant Colonel Schilling, formerly of the Seventy-ninth Royal Grenadiers, and currently on loan to the American Air Force. After identifying himself, the voice explained that he and several colleagues had found nine intercontinental ballistic missiles, with nuclear warheads, that were still in their silos. Considering the state of the world, the good Colonel felt certain that no one in the United States wanted more death and destruction. His proposal was for an ungodly amount of gold, diamonds, platinum, and electronic components to be delivered to the missile base where he was holed up. In return, he and his colleagues would not launch the rockets. In the event that America did not comply, the Colonel guaranteed he'd reassign each missile to an undestroyed area in the United States, one of which was Marysville.

Shortly after the voice of Death and Doom had identified himself and made his purpose known, the voice of Hope came on the air. The new voice identified himself as William Wesley of the National Security Council, but we could just call him Bill. He sounded like a young kid who had just made contact with a new radio pal. He chit-chatted for hours about weather, war, his family, government policy before the war, and anything except the voice of Death and Doom's demands. Whenever the voice of Doom pressed for information, reaction, or compliance, the voice of Hope would say everything was being taken care of by the Security Council and then switch to another irrelevant topic of discussion.

The whole drama was like listening to a radio soap opera, except the stakes were additional death and destruction. Towards the end of the drama, the anxiety and frustration became maddening. The voice of Hope kept babbling on about ridiculous dribble and the voice of Death and Doom kept getting angrier and more strained.

When the deadline set by the voice of Death and Doom was reached, the radio drama ended. While attempting to change the target setting in one of the missile's guidance systems, it blew up. One, small, underground nuclear explosion that obliterated the missile complex and destroyed the other warheads, as well as Lt. Col. Schilling and his crew.

William Wesley came on an hour after the last words of the drama had been spoken. In a calm voice he explained what had happened. He apologized to all the citizens who had endured the last ninety-six hours of the nightmare. He spoke at some length explaining that the Security Council knew all along what would happen if the guidance system were tampered with, but there was no way to give that information out without tipping off Colonel Schilling and his men.

"Now the crisis is over and the danger is passed. We must not lose sight of our goal to build a new country." The voice of Hope told his national radio audience.

Everyone here seems mentally exhausted by the ordeal. It was as if we had all held our breath for four days. No one was sure how the situation would end, or how it would affect us directly, but we all had to re-experience the fear of nuclear death and destruction. In Marysville there had been a genuine panic when people tried to evacuate the city. The whole situation has raised questions around the country. Could it happen again?

Are there still weapons in other countries? Will we always have to live in fear of nuclear bombs? A pall, or spectre, has been cast over the community again. People feel that they were punished for feeling good and starting to enjoy life.

JULY 20

We returned from our regular fishing trip late this afternoon. It was a quiet trip. Everyone on the boat, like everyone at the community, was quiet. People only talk when it's necessary, there is no good old fashioned bullshit!

While at the coast, we came across two other fishing boats. Both were from farther north, near Ft. Bragg. Both boats were smaller than Survivor I, but they were well made and equipped for open ocean fishing. We talked briefly while passing. The captains of the two boats said food was running out up north, so fishing was necessary to feed the survivors.

Radiation in the northernmost part of the state, and in Washington and Oregon, has not diminished as it has in other areas. Prevailing winds continue to carry fallout in from other sources. Many think the fallout is blowing in from Russia. How ironic to be killed by radioactive fallout from our own missile warheads.

JULY 22

The mood here seems to be relaxing. My father has always said you teach by example. Sam, Shellie, Nellie, Donna, dad, mom and I have gone throughout the community to talk and laugh with each other and other survivors. It is hoped that people will see that lightning doesn't strike you for laughing, or talking, or feeling good. More and more people are feeling less anxious about being punished or rebuked for having a positive attitude.

JULY 24

I am a whole fifteen and a half; I have survived a nuclear

holocaust, killed men face to face, observed suffering beyond my wildest comprehension. I was not prepared for the news I got today. Dad is dying of leukemia.

I bust my ass trying to make people smile. Dad goes grey trying to help people survive. Others work overtime trying to make life better for their fellow man. The end result of all this self effacement is shit. Useless shit!

I've watched my father for seven months do everything possible to help everyone but himself. He has lost weight, his hair has turned white, he doesn't sleep at night and he is weak compared to the man who took his family into the mines a half year ago. He is dying! My father is dying!

Dr. Frantz and dad came by the living quarters tonight, made small talk and nonchalantly mentioned that dad has leukemia. They tried to pass it off as nothing, but that was bullshit, too. Prior to the war his chances were slim. Now, with little or no modern medicine, his chances are little to none.

"Screw it! Just screw it!"

JULY 26

My father is the greatest man I have ever known, or read about, or heard about. I realize my feelings are extremely biased, but I'd put his accomplishments and achievements against anyone I can think of. His name may never appear in any history book, he will never be the hero of any major novel, but he is a bigger than life hero to me and to many of the people in this community who have had dealings with him.

He is dying. Dr. Frantz says a year at best——six months most likely. The last two months, or so, are going to be excruciating pain and suffering. A wholly unjust end to a hero.

I am experiencing a bitterness I've never known. There is no way I can see, feel, or rationalize justification for what's happening to my father. There are so many individuals in this community who have done little and contributed nothing. They could die tomorrow and no one would notice or care. There are people who have been exposed to ten times the radiation of dad. Why should he be the one? Why should he die? There are so many people who owe their existence to my father, so many good situations that exist because my father cared. How can fate, God, karma, or whatever, be so cruel?

I have told my mother and father that as long as he is alive I will be his arms, legs, eyes, ears or voice. I am dedicated to making my father's last months on this planet, tolerable. He says he doesn't need or want my help, so I will be discreet, but I will be there.

JULY 28

Something right out of the old west movies showed up today, a man dressed all in black, riding a huge black horse, carrying a Bible and quoting scripture. It would have been very funny except the man was very serious. He perched himself on a short cement wall, between the main college building and the living quarters, and began a hellfire and brimstone sermon. He told everyone who would stop to listen that the death and destruction that is all around them was their own fault. It was their reward for having led sinning lives. Now they were doomed to this hell on earth.

Most people stopped and listened long enough to satisfy their curiosity, then went on about their business. A few individuals who were offended by the preacher's remarks, made comments or asked questions. Two older women, who had lost everyone and everything during the war, spent most of the day sitting in front of the preacher. Betty and Lou sat and nodded agreement and even gave out with a few amens. When the late meal was served, the two women brought the preacher to the main dining hall. He ate quietly with everyone else. After dinner he spoke and prayed quietly with the two sisters. Afterward he went outside and bedded down by his horse.

I heard a few people talking about the preacher. Some were saying he should be run off and not allowed to upset people. Others said to ignore him and he'd go away. The general consensus was that he is hurting the morale of the community.

JULY 30

Dad and I spent the entire day on the boat, preparing it for tomorrow's trip to the coast. Dad outwardly appears fine, but I know he tires easily.

The weather has been extremely cold the past few days. A stiff breeze out of the northwest has been blowing the clouds swiftly across the dark grey sky. There are white caps on the river and Sam says the ocean may be really rough. We are going to go to the entrance of San Francisco Bay and see how the ocean looks before we actually commit the boat to a long, hard trip and poor fishing conditions.

Dad and Sam are concerned that during the regular winter months fishing may become impossible due to bad ocean and weather conditions. With fish the main food staple here, people would starve. Sam is suggesting that the boat begin making two trips a week for the next couple of months. This would allow the community to stockpile fish through non-fishing months. Jerry has suggested construction of a second boat to double the intake.

AUGUST 3

Our last trip to the ocean was very uneventful. The water was rough, but we caught a good haul of fish. We also saw some whales. Sam said they were humpbacks.

The weather has gotten steadily worse. It has rained twice. Once yesterday and a little this morning. The rain is cold and could become snow very easily. How severe the cold gets will determine how difficult life in the community will be. We can ration food; we can regulate the heat to a certain extent; but eventually we will run out of food and our heat and electricity will fail.

Dad has suggested to our newly elected representatives that an alternate living quarters be developed inside the coal mines where our family survived previously. He has devised a construction plan that would create comfortable living conditions for an indefinite length of time. The plan provides sleeping accommodations, feeding areas, water for cleaning and cooking, a central heating system that is more efficient than what we now have, large greenhouses and more. As dad has pointed out, the mines provide a natural shelter with water and space. All we have to do is add plumbing and electricity.

The new council will assign a construction crew to begin work at the mines as soon as possible. The idea of returning to the mines bothers me, but it might be better than staying out where the cold could kill me.

AUGUST 5

It hasn't rained and the wind has died down some. There is a lot of activity around here. Workers are preparing to take building materials to the mines, the raising and fitting of a new fishing boat has begun, additional solar stills are being constructed to produce methanol for fuel, preparations for the next fishing trip are underway. An expedition by boat to the Farallon Islands and along the coast, south, is being planned, and Nellie is teaching school daily with the help of Shellie and me.

Dad, Jerry, Sam and I are going to take a boat ride out to the Farallon Islands to check the sea life and bird populations. Most chicken and duck populations have died, even on the north coast. Sam thinks we might be able to substitute poultry and eggs from sea birds. On our return trip we are going south to Point Sur, and then follow the coast north to San Francisco Bay. This will allow us to look for any resources that may be usable.

AUGUST 7

Tomorrow we leave for our Farallon trip. The boat is loaded up and ready to go. The weather is holding fair and we should have a good trip.

I spent yesterday helping Jerry and another man locate another boat. We found a second boat near the boat harbor at Bridgehead. The boat harbor was located next to where the Antioch Bridge used to cross the river. The boat we found is in ten feet of water and in relatively good condition. The boat crew will try to raise it in the next day or so. Jerry already has an alcohol burning engine constructed that will fit the boat. With the additional boat we can double our food resources.

AUGUST 9

I am sitting on the fantail of Survivor I. We have been anchored off the Farallon Islands since noon yesterday. Sam has been ashore talking with two scientists who have been living on the island. They had been living here when the war happened. They decided they were better off on the island than ashore. They have a great deal of scientific equipment, a boat, and unlimited supply of food resources.

The men have told Sam that the effects of radiation are just now becoming evident. Immediately after the missile warheads fell, the bird populations diminished greatly. Many of the seals and sea lions disappeared. Slowly the birds and mammals began reappearing in greater numbers, but many are deformed and many cannot survive the harsh environment.

We are going to take some birds back with us that the scientists have been raising since birth. It is hoped that we will be able to domesticate an entire flock. The eggs and the birds themselves could become a food source.

Tomorrow morning we are heading south, then east. It

is planned that we will encounter the coast near Big Sur. Dad wants to see if there is any forest land still producing trees south of New Los Medanos. We will survey the coast between Point Sur and San Francisco Bay. We are looking for anything that could be of use to us, and for any survivors who could give us information about the area.

AUGUST 10

We returned home last night after a long and disheartening trip along the California coast. There was nothing good to report from our search. Nuclear fires blackened everything. There are no buildings, plants, animals, or people. Monterey Bay is a giant mud hole. All the land we could see is barren and desolate.

Unfortunately, that's the good news. The bad news is roaches. Billions of them. Just north of Santa Cruz Jerry spotted movement on the hill above the beach. As we neared the beach for a closer inspection, Sam gave out with a short scream. She had been watching the hill with binoculars. She was the first to see the movement closely——a mound of roaches, twenty feet high and a hundred feet long. A teaming, living mass of cockroaches. Some of the roaches had mutated and were as large as my hand. Most were the good old, get in the cookie jar, kitchen variety, but the numbers were mind boggling.

We observed the movement for an hour. It appears that the whole mound of roaches is moving. It looks like a giant hill on rollers as it slowly moves north.

Sam went ashore briefly where the roaches had already passed. She made some quick observations, then returned to the boat. She said it appears that the mound is feeding and eating itself. Thousands of roaches are born every hour and thousands die. The dead, weak, or injured are eaten by the rest. Whenever the mound passes over something edible, it consumes the food source. Radioactivity appears to have no effect on the roaches.

AUGUST 11

The report on the roaches seems to have created major concern here. Immediately after the war, roaches and beetles had been in evidence everywhere around this area. Some survivors had even taken to eating them. Within the last two months, the insect population had diminished greatly. Now the concern is that the roaches have gone somewhere to unite into a giant eating machine.

Two groups have been set up. One is the original insect search and destroy team. It has been defunct for months. The other group is going to travel to the coast to observe and test the hill of roaches. Emil, Frank's friend, has volunteered to head the coast group. He looks very young with wispy blond hair and pale white skin. He is slight of stature and rather timid. He is older than he looks.

Dr. Bronson told the school children to go out around the community and find insects, any kind, and bring them to him to examine. He is going to test the insects here to see if they have undergone any changes, and determine if they can be killed or controlled with conventional methods.

AUGUST 12

This morning we held an entomology class for all the students. We showed them the differences between bugs, insects, spiders, butterflies, bees, ants and beetles. When we were sure they had the basics, we armed all the young kids with jars, small boxes, paper envelopes and anything else that could be used to hold a bug or two.

The rest of the day looked like a giant scavenger hunt. Many adults, who heard what the kids were doing, joined in the hunt. Some tried to catch insects themselves, while some just showed the kids good places to look.

By evening mealtime several hundred insects had been rounded up and brought to the classroom. Dad is going to assist Dr. Bronson in trying to categorize the various finds. Most of the captured specimens were in good shape. Some got a little mangled, or smashed, by the enthusiastic young hunters.

AUGUST 14

A convoy of military trucks drove up today. The trucks were loaded with food, small machines, medicine, some electrical supplies and hand tools.

The officer in charge of the convoy was all military. Each of the six trucks had a driver and an armed rider. The men all said, "sir", and saluted. The major gave orders, did all the talking, and conducted business without smiles or jokes.

After all the materials had been unloaded and carefully stored, dad invited the major and his men into the college cafeteria for food and drink. While the soldiers ate, dad questioned them about where they'd been and what they had seen.

The major told dad that eight months ago he had been a new second lieutenant in the Nevada National Guard. After the war he was one of only several officers in the state. At first the guardsmen only acted as policemen and kept the peace. Now they are in charge of distribution of all supplies. He said that great collection and distribution centers are being established in certain strategic locations across the country. These centers collect available resources from the surrounding areas and also receive shipments from other parts of the country. The job of the regional centers is to spread the supplies out equally over as large an area as will benefit the most survivors.

The major, whose name is Jonathan Lyle, of Elko, Nevada, wants dad to take him to the coast to meet with survivors there. The military wants to build an airstrip at the coast. They want to establish a large fishing industry and transport the fresh fish to other areas of the country. The major says similar areas are being established on the Texas Gulf, the Florida Keys, the New England Coast, and the Great Lakes. The leading scientists feel that seafood must now become our main food source.

This evening, after Major Lyle gave final instructions to his men, I invited him to come sit by the radio. I told him it was our biggest form of entertainment. He said it was in most of the communities he has visited.

We sat quietly for an hour and listened as Frank talked to various radio operators around the state. We listened to conversations in other states that were too far away to communicate with. It was an unusually dull night for listening. Major Lyle and I made small talk about the community and its inhabitants. Then, as if he just thought of it, or noticed, he asked why I didn't look like other survivors. I laughed at his seemingly sudden revelation and explained how the family had avoided most radiation by living in the mines. I concluded my short explanation by telling him of dad's illness. Not wanting to inflict a bad mood on the major, or myself, I quickly changed the conversation and asked him how he had survived for the past eight months.

Major Jonathan Lyle, age twenty-five, graduated from the University of Nevada at Las Vegas with a degree in engineering. He had been involved in ROTC while in college and that had led to his commission as a Second Lieutenant in the National Guard. He had been working in construction for the last year and a half to make enough money to do some traveling in Europe and to return to school for an advanced degree. He had been doing finishing work on a large concrete basement when the missiles came. He stayed inside the basement for nearly a month. He came out when the water and food he had was gone. When he came out of hiding he made his way to the nearest National Guard armory for supplies. When he got there, he found a poorly organized, makeshift, relief shelter and twenty sick guardsmen. He organized the area and the situation as best he could, then made contact with other survivor groups. For his efforts the National Guard made him a major.

For the past two months Major Lyle has been in charge of the distribution center in Nevada. Supply convoys have gone to Washington, Oregon, Idaho, and eastern parts of California. Major Lyle took personal command of this convoy because his superiors want him to contact the coast survivors regarding the building of an airstrip and establishment of a major fishing community.

I left Major Lyle by the radio at about eleven and went to my sleeping quarters.

AUGUST 15

Sam and dad are making a special trip to the coast. They will do some fishing and take Major Lyle to Stewart's Point. He is going to meet with elected officials and explain the scientist's plan.

On the return trip they will check the San Francisco beaches for Emil and his group. That is where the boat dropped the group off. When they completed their observations, they were suppose to return to the beach and wait to be picked up by the boat.

Major Lyle will be be leaving tomorrow for Nevada. He says he will probably be returning in the next couple of weeks to talk with dad and go to the coast. He is going to bring a load of books and school supplies for our little school. He says he is really impressed with how organized we are here. He told dad that there is less cohesiveness and organization in areas that did not receive any missile hits.

AUGUST 16

Major Lyle left this morning with his trucks and men. He said his meeting at the coast was very successful.

I will be looking forward to his return visit. I enjoyed

talking to him. He reminds me a lot of Harry. I wish Harry were still alive and here to share and help in rebuilding the world. I miss Harry and I will miss Major Lyle until he returns.

Dad and Sam did not see Emil or his group. They will check again day after tomorrow.

I am going to go with Jerry tomorrow and help raise the new boat we've found. Jerry has patched the hull and we will pump out the water. Sam and Jerry have been collecting materials, fittings and equipment to fix up the boat. With the new alcohol burning engine, the boat could be ready for its maiden voyage in a week.

AUGUST 17

The boat raising turned into a community event. It started when Nellie and Shellie brought a group of students from the school. Some workers saw the kids walking off toward the waterfront, where Jerry had towed the submerged boat hulk, and decided to find out where they were going. A few of the elderly around the complex saw the workers leaving their jobs early and went to see why. This group coupled with the ten or so members of the boat crew gave us an audience of fifty or more people.

It took about two hours to pump the water out and raise the boat. The original name on the back of the boat was "Escape". Jerry joked at how appropriately the forty foot Bayliner had been named. As soon as the boat was afloat the crowd started cheering. The boat crew got on board and immediately began the refitting.

It is good to see people working and trying, concerned and involved. For so long this community looked like a home for wayward zombies. The people were all listless and sickly. Now people seem alive. They walk instead of shuffle. Their heads are up, instead of down. The sickly have died off. We have lost over fifty people since the community was formed. Those of us left are strong. Even dad, who is dying, walks briskly and speaks clearly, and has bright clear eyes. People's clothes are no longer rags. Everyone is clean. No one goes hungry and everyone gets plenty of exercise and sleep. The ravages of radiation still linger as skin blotches, missing hair, missing teeth, and scars, but they are less conspicuous on clean, warmly dressed, smiling people.

AUGUST 18

The fishing boat returned from the coast this morning. There was still no sign of Emil's group. Dad and Dr. Bronson are worried. They don't think it should have taken this long for the group to observe and examine the roaches.

Our regularly scheduled fishing trip is tomorrow. We are going to look for Emil's group in the morning and on our return trip. If we do not see them tomorrow, a search party will be organized.

Frank received a radio message from Major Lyle today. He told Frank that the convoy had made it back to Nevada safely. He also said to thank everyone for their hospitality.

AUGUST 20

On the return trip from fishing yesterday, we made a search of the beaches as far south as Pacifica. There was no sign of Emil or any member of his group. It is amazing how the wind and sea have reclaimed the beach areas and the surrounding land. The areas that had, only months ago, been covered with the black and gray ash of nuclear destruction are now covered with blowing sand and sprouting grasses. Patches of ice plant are emerging through the sand drifts.

Where buildings and other structures stood great splotches of brown and orange are appearing. It is the rusting and oxidation of steel and iron. Different plants, grasses, molds and cacti are trying to grow amid the radioactive carnage.

Tomorrow Jerry is going to drop Frank, Larry and Sam and myself off near Pacifica. We are going to travel south in the direction Emil and the three volunteers were to have gone.

AUGUST 23

The community is busy arming itself for a war against the oncoming roaches. Two days ago we found the lone survivor of Emil's group. Sean is an eighteen year old. All of his friends and relatives were killed in the war. He has been very helpful throughout the community. It was no surprise when he volunteered to go with Emil to investigate the roaches.

Our search team found Sean about five miles south of where we landed. He was unconscious, lying face down in the sand. His leg is broken and he had dragged himself for two days. He is suffering from shock and exposure. After Dr. Frantz treated him, he was able to tell what had happened to the rest of the group.

Emil and the three men had found the roach hill the day after they were taken ashore. From what Sam had told them, they determined that the roaches had moved nearly twenty miles. They observed the mound for two full days. On the third day Emil decided that there was nothing to learn, by observation, that Sam hadn't already guessed. He figured a few specimens would be the best approach.

Emil and another group member, named John, went down the hill they had been watching from. They took two mason jars to put specimens in. From the hill Sean and the remaining volunteer, Lee, could see their partners and the roaches. They also saw something that Emil and John could not see. As the two men approached the mound, two columns of roaches moved out from the mound. From the hill it appeared as two giant pinchers moving out and away, but not becoming detached.

Sean and Lee realized that the two arms of roaches were moving out to encircle their unsuspecting companions.

The two men started yelling and screaming for the others to return, but the hum of the roach mound and the distance made it difficult to hear and impossible to understand.

As Emil and John stood before the roach mound, looking back at their two screaming companions, they were encircled by the two quickly closing arms. It was at that point that Emil discerned the frantic gyrations of Sean and Lee, but it was too late. Within minutes the roaches were on Emil and John. They stomped and flailed wildly, possibly killing a thousand bugs each, but in the end, their screaming, writhing bodies fell to the ground and waited for the fast moving hungry mound of roaches to completely engulf them.

Lee was in hysterics and Sean was violently ill. They had helplessly witnessed the gross death of their friends. Sean regained his composure and tried to calm Lee down. He pushed Lee to the ground and pinned him by straddling his chest. He yelled at Lee until he gained his attention. Then he soothed him by saying it was time for them to leave. He explained that they must make it back to the beach and wait for the boat.

When the two young men were ready to leave they had their second horrifying shock. The base of the hill they were on was surrounded by roaches. Two additional columns had moved out from the mound and encircled the hill. Unable to cope with the shock, Lee bolted from the hill. He sprinted down the slope farthest from the mound. When he reached the twenty foot wide barrier of roaches he leaped into the air. He easily cleared the roaches, but his forward momentum caused him to lose his balance. He rolled forward, head over heels, and landed motionless five yards from the scurrying roaches. At first the roaches made no move towards Lee. Sean watched in silence as Lee began to stir. As soon as the roaches detected the movement, the whole wall rushed Lee. Mercifully he had not regained consciousness sufficiently to be fully aware of the roach attack. There were no screams or fighting, just a few spasmodic nervous jerks, then nothing. He was covered by thousands of roaches.

Sean stood on the top of the hill for over an hour. The

roaches surrounding the hill never came up. When the mound reached the hill it just seemed to flow around the base. Sean got a large stick and began digging a large hole. By late afternoon he had dug a three foot pit in the soft sandy soil, big enough to lie in. The group had previously observed that the roach mound ate only about an inch below the surface it passed over. Sean figured he could bury himself a foot or so deep and remain buried through the night. If the roaches came over the hill, he might go undetected and survive.

As the sun began setting on the coast, Sean entered his pit and scooped a foot of soil onto his body. With only his face, shoulders and arms exposed, he used his jacket to construct a tent over his face and then proceeded to cover his head and shoulders. When he had scooped all the soil he could reach into the pit and onto his head, he worked his hands and arms down into the loose dirt. The weight of the soil was oppressive, but not unbearable.

Sean did not know how long he was buried in the pit before he heard the humming of the roaches increase. Shortly, the weight of the soil on him began getting heavier. At first the weight was only slight, then it began to grow. Sean found it difficult to breathe due to the weight on his chest and face. Sean lost consciousness soon after the roaches covered the hill and his hiding place. When Sean regained consciousness, he could not hear the hum of the roaches. He moved one of his arms carefully. It was difficult getting it extricated from solid soil that had been packed down around it. Once his arm was free, he brushed soil from his jacket that covered his face. Slowly he lifted the jacket and peered up at the fog moving quickly in from the sea. He took big breaths of the cold sea air and slowly worked his body out of the dirt and into a sitting position. In the dark he saw several dead roaches in the soil on his jacket. The roaches had come within inches of finding and eating him. The thought so revolted and disgusted him that he jumped out of the shallow pit and began brushing dirt and any possible insects from his body. His body was tingling from lack of circulation and he imagined it to be bugs. In his fear and exhilaration he began running towards the ocean a quarter mile away. Fifty yards from his objective he found himself in mid air. In the darkness he did not see the ravine running to the beach. The thirty foot drop was bad, but the sudden stop on craggy boulders is what broke his leg.

Sean had immobilized the leg as best he could. He had crawled many miles, dragging his swollen and painful leg before we found him. His thin, dark hair seemed almost dark grey and his dark Mexican skin had become pale and ashen. His dark brown eyes are no longer fiery and they seem to be framed in a much older man's face. The shock of his ordeal is incomprehensible to me.

Tomorrow we will attack the roaches and avenge Sean, Lee, John and Emil.

AUGUST 25

Somewhere in the back of my mind I have a recollection of hearing Marlin Perkins, or William Conrad, narrate a television show on cockroaches. It was one of the Public Broadcasting shows that tells you the intimate sex lives of bugs, snakes, snails or tzetze flies. In this program I'm sure I heard the narrator say that roaches had been around for millions of years and would probably be one of the species that would survive even a nuclear war. Little did they know.

We fought the first roach war yesterday. I think we lost. We burned several million roaches, but we couldn't kill them all and we couldn't stop the mound. We threw Molotov cocktails and sprayed methanol on the fire with hand pumped sprayers, but the mound is so thick and so dense that we only burned the outside layer. The burning mound lit up the evening sky as the boat headed back to New Los Medanos, but the roaches were not destroyed.

Dad has contacted Major Lyle and scientists about the roaches. Major Lyle is coming down with flame throwers and white phosphorus grenades. He thinks the increased heat will work into the center of the mound. Our next battle will be near South San Francisco, day after tomorrow.

AUGUST 28

The war with roaches is over! At least in our area anyway. However, other areas have now reported roach mounds, smaller but growing. The mounds seem to develop in remote, devastated areas and then start moving.

It took two full days of burning and bombing the mound in South San Francisco to destroy it. The carnage began with grenades of white phosphorus and thermite being tossed onto the mound. Then fire bombs were detonated after the mound had moved over them. The mound slowly shrunk. Layer after layer of roach bodies were burned off with flame throwers. In the end a mound twenty feet in diameter and three feet high was burned, scattered and burned again. I'm sure a few thousand roaches scurried off and hid. A new mound could arise in the future, but for now the score is people one, roaches zero.

Major Lyle returned to Nevada this morning to give the scientists there a report on the situation. He'll be back next week. He and dad are going to go to the coast for two days to pick a site for an airstrip and a fish factory that will contain a processing and packaging plant and a fish hatchery.

When Major Lyle and dad have finished at the coast they are going to the mines and spend time there working on a project dad has been planning.

At both locations I will have ample opportunity to talk with Major Lyle. I'm looking forward to it.

AUGUST 29

Everything is getting back to normal now that the roach scare is over. I think we all had a science fiction mentality and thought the roaches would be invincible. They were scary and menacing, but they were not invincible.

All the kids are back to learning reading, writing and math. There is no more bug collecting, though I'm sure they all learned a great deal about insects from the experience. Shellie and Nellie have invited dad and Teddy to come and give a class on our new form of government. I will be sure to be in class that day. I want to hear how they explain the subtle differences between our former democracy and our growing socialistic state and federal government.

Work on the new boat has been suspended for a few days. Now the entire boat/fishing committee is at work preparing to launch the Escape on its first river trip. The alcohol engine is the last obstacle to overcome. Jerry has been solely responsible for building and installing the new engine. Dr. Bronson and Jerry brought the new engine design back from the scientist meeting in Nevada. Even the lubricants for this engine are made from alcohol.

The initial test of the new boat is scheduled for the day after tomorrow.

AUGUST 30

I just became aware of a curious phenomenon. When we first came out of the mines and started establishing this community, I was a peer, an adult. I was admired for my stamina, my strength, and my health. No one here questioned my ability, or my age. I carried out the duties assigned only to adults. No one ever said, "You're too young," or "You're a girl."

Today I went down to the river to help in the launching of the new boat. In the past I have been an accepted member of the boat crew. When the boat was ready for its maiden trip, I was asked by Jerry and Sam to stay on the shore with "the other kids". Suddenly I'm not an adult!

Now that the health and strength of the adult survivors

has greatly improved and they can now do a full day's work, I'm relegated back to "child" status. I think I'm more amazed by the whole change of attitude than any-thing else. My initial reaction was to stand and stare in open-mouthed astonishment. My reaction from now on will be to assert my position maturely. I will not allow myself to act, or be treated, as a child.

If that doesn't work, I'll throw a tantrum.

SEPTEMBER 1

The boat, the new engine and the alcohol based lubricants are all successful. Tomorrow the New Los Medanos fishing fleet will leave for the coast to catch twice the fish it has in the past.

I spoke with Sam last night after the Escape was put to bed. I told her that I was offended at being referred to as a "child", and I was hurt that she had demonstrated that attitude towards me. She was quiet for a long time before she put her long slender arm across my shoulders. She confided that what she was going to say was between her and I and not to be repeated again. I told her I was adult enough to be trusted. She laughed and then got up from where we were sitting. She stood directly in front of me.

"Your father, Gene, has asked everyone to stop treating you like an adult. He has requested that you slowly be relieved of all duties except the school. He wants you to spend more time with him and your family."

I started to smile, thinking she had made up the story to relieve my frustration, but then I realized she was serious.

"Why?" I stammered, rather incredulously.

"Gene is dying. He doesn't know how much time he has left. He wants to be with you and your sisters as much as possible. Humor him, Jessie, you have a lot of living to do. He doesn't."

With that Sam left the dock and headed for Survivor I and Jerry. I sat quietly by myself for awhile, then I left for the college.

SEPTEMBER 3

I have been up at the mines since yesterday morning. Dad told me he needed my help with the project he is working on there.

Dad and I walked up to the mines and I was floored by what I found. On the tops of the hills there are many wind mills. In the large caverns near the entrance ways are stills for alcohol production and green houses with different gardens and different kinds of food plants. Further into the mines the passageways have been paved with cement. The cement has water pipes running through it. Water can be heated and pumped through the pipes to warm the walkways and the tunnels.

Throughout the mines there is construction of living quarters, workshops, feeding areas, and bathroom facilities. There is a cement factory, a giant storage area, and a cavern-size refrigeration area being completed.

Dad gave me a complete tour with high points explained. Then he took me to a medium-size cavern and said this would be used as a classroom. He told me he wanted me to design how it should be laid out and what should be inside. I spent yesterday and today drawing a plan for the eighty by one hundred foot cavern with forty foot ceiling.

SEPTEMBER 4

A huge helicopter came swooping in from the east today and landed in front of the college. There were several engineers, two scientists and Major Lyle.

The group met with dad, Dr. Bronson, Jerry, Sam, Frank, Donna and the elected council members. After several hours the engineers, scientists, dad, Major Lyle and Sam went out to board the helicopter. I asked dad if I could go with him to the coast. He smiled at Sam and then asked Major Lyle if there would be enough room. Major Lyle said that the CH-53 had plenty of room.

I went and collected a change of clothes and told mom I was going with dad. I also told Nellie I'd be away for a couple of days and that she was in charge of the school. She was very businesslike and professional. She assured me that everything would be fine. I laughed quietly to myself at the attitude she puts on for the kids at the school. She has mellowed a lot since we came down from the mines. When she is not in school she runs and plays and laughs like the little girl she is. I'm glad.

The helicopter ride took only thirty minutes. We lifted off, made a wide circle over the community, and then flew northwest across the river. It seemed we were never more than a few hundred feet above the ground, even when we cleared the mountains near the coast. The scientists never left the side door. They were all taking notes, pointing at sights on the ground and talking excitedly. Apparently they have not seen the devastation that exists here. Major Lyle says it is different in each area—different terrains, different climates, different vegetation, and the degree of missile hits and radiation all contribute to different phenomena in each area.

At the coast we were shown to our sleeping quarters in a local motel, then we were driven in a battered police van to a meeting hall. We spent the entire day in meetings. I stayed closest to Sam. She was the ocean expert and fish was the only area I could feel comfortable talking about. Several times during the day Sam was asked important questions that required long, involved, technical answers. After she had given her response she would look at me and ask if I agreed. I would give a moment's contemplation and then say, "I'm sure I couldn't have put it better."

SEPTEMBER 5

Last night after dinner Major Lyle and I went for a walk on the nearby rocky beach. We watched a hazy sunset and felt the bite of a frosty fog that came in from the restless ocean. We sat on a large flat boulder that faced the water and talked late into the night. I wish I could write that it was a romantic episode, but it was not. When Major Lyle discerned my questioning about a wife, a girl-friend, his future, etc., he put everything in its proper perspective.

Major Lyle told me he was flattered by my interest in him. He said in another time and place it might be dif-ferent, but not now, and not here. He has no desire to have a wife, or girlfriend, to worry about. He has even less desire to bring children into this world now. He said we met because of the war. If there had been no war we would have never met. Our lives, our situations, and our thinking would all be different. He feels his only purpose now is to help others and to try and restore the country to what it was before the war——maybe even make it better.

I'm disappointed. Maybe even a bit put down, but I under-stand his reasoning and his feelings. I guess I'm just feeling my teenage hormones and acting out the desperation I feel about the possibility of growing to full womanhood and never knowing all the things I assumed I would know.

Before returning to our quarters for the night, Major Lyle gave me a hug and told me he hoped all my dreams would be fulfilled someday by a truly decent young man, a young man who was deserving of the strength and beauty I pos-sess. He may have only been trying to cheer me, but the sentiment and the compliment were the greatest I can ever remember.

Sam and I spent most of today near the water talking

with the scientists. Dr. Eller and Dr. Anderson will be in charge of establishing the fishery here. Both are fifty plus years old, grey haired and extremely studious. They are constantly taking and comparing notes. I have never known two more totally engrossed people. It is as if the world is a giant experiment and they are collecting data for a major report. I would love to ask them questions, but they never have time.

SEPTEMBER 7

We all flew back from the coast yesterday. The scientists requested a route over San Francisco so that they could see first hand the havoc wreaked there. I'm sure it was the highlight of their careers.

The helicopter landed at the community early in the morning. Jerry ferried us all up to the mines. It took two trips. I rode up with Dr. Eller and Dr. Anderson. I told them how we had lived in the mines and how the area had looked when we first came out. The hills now are covered with a yellow-green grass and a yellow-brown moss. The hills look like food left in a refrigerator too long. They look stale and moldy. The scientists were fascinated and said they would like to return soon with a botanist to study the new flora. Dad and the engineers spent all day walking the mines and discussing ways of building, reinforcing, tunneling and expanding. Dad has made a building materials request list for the engineers to take back with them.

Last night I asked dad why all the building was going on at the mines. He told me he thinks we will need the additional space eventually, and that if the winter is as harsh as it could be, the structures at the college may not be adequate.

SEPTEMBER 8

Major Lyle, the scientists and the engineers all flew back

to Nevada this morning. The engineers are going to try to requisition additional supplies for the project at the coast. All the additional materials will be channeled to our construction at the mines.

Dad has started crews digging new tunnels into the sandstone walls of the existing caves. The sand will be used in cement and fill, the new caverns will provide space for members of the community. At present the mines could not support the entire population of New Los Medanos.

SEPTEMBER 10

When we are little, our parents are like giants, super humans. They know everything, they can do anything, they are perfect. We put our parents on pedestals and worship them. As we grow older, and less dependent, that pedestal gets a little smaller, a little less high. Each year, as our ability increases and our parent's influence lessens, the pedestal shrinks. Depending on how quickly we mature and begin to form our own opinions, the pedestal will eventually disappear. At that point we become equals. In some instances, it is a gentle transition. In others it becomes a major confrontation. The turbulence of this transition, or awakening, is determined by how prepared the parent and the child are to deal with it.

I was not ready. Mom was even less prepared than I. The result is I'm now living on the Escape and mom refuses to talk to me. Oddly, dad has not attempted to intervene and is totally noncommittal to either side.

I love my mother dearly, but I have known how to manipulate her since I was eleven. I've often, before and after the war, played mom against dad, mom against Nellie, mom against my step dad. Knowing how easily she was manipulated made me lose a little respect for her, the pedestal got a little shorter. Since the war I have undergone many changes. I am physically and mentally stronger. My decision making skills are good and my responsibility level is beyond question. I think I am as mature and responsible as any "adult" I know. Mom cannot accept that at fifteen years and nine months, I am capable of making adult decisions.

If there had been no war and I were living in Antioch and attending school, I probably would not question mom's decisions. I might try to work around them, but I wouldn't question her authority. She's just going to have to change her thinking. She cannot judge me and my actions by values from a prewar world.

The request I made that started all this was to move to the coast and learn from the engineers and scientists who will be building the airport, fish packaging plant, and fish hatchery. I think the information I could learn there could benefit people here and all over California.

SEPTEMBER 12

I was at the mines this morning trying to explain to one of the construction workers that I wanted a balcony built high on the wall of the classroom. He couldn't understand why I would want a balcony in a classroom, so I drew him a picture of a balcony that would allow access to the book shelves high up on the sandstone walls. He went off scratching his head, but I think he got the idea. We're trying to use all available space.

When I had finished talking with the construction worker and he left, mom walked slowly into the cavern. She walked around the large sandstone room, now cluttered with building materials, and quietly eyed the space's potential. After a few minutes of silence she stopped in front of me.

"The place sure looks different since my last visit." She said with a slight smile.

I laughed and asked her what she was doing here. She told me she rode up with Jerry to see me.

She came to me and gave me a big hug. As she did she said she was sorry for being so protective. I suddenly felt very small. I had humiliated my mother into apologizing to me. I had a sudden desire to be anyplace but here. I felt tears well up in my eyes. I returned my mother's hug.

"I'm sorry I've been a little bitch." I whispered to her earnestly.

We separated and I saw that she also had tears in her eyes. It suddenly occurred to me that though I had matured, grown, and experienced things beyond my years, I was not an adult. I had never given and sacrificed the way a parent does for a child, the way my mother had done for me.

We spoke together for a long time in the noise and dust of the mines. We parted as equals and as friends. I apologized for not understanding her point of view. She apologized for selfishly wanting me close to her and the girls.

I love my mother!!

SEPTEMBER 13

When next week's fishing trip leaves for the coast I will be going along to spend the next three months there. I will be staying with an older woman who is a friend of Jonah's. He has been staying there when he is not in Marysville. He has not tried to rebuild his house since it was burned by the terrorists.

I have talked at great length with both mom and dad. Mom says she will miss me and hopes I'm not wasting my time by going to the coast to learn about fish and the ocean. Dad is not real happy about my going away and says for me to stay in touch with him and mom regularly. I have promised to send letters down with the fishing boats every week. Dad knows it is important for me to learn and do something useful. The sea will be the greatest resource for food, salt, fertilizer and other materials we will need to rebuild our planet.

I will spend the rest of this week preparing for my trip. Several other community members are also preparing to go to the coast. They are going because the construction there will provide jobs. The military and scientists have also promised food, medicine, doctors and living quarters to all who work on the project.

SEPTEMBER 16

Teddy came back from Marysville yesterday. He gave a report to the community last night on the progress of our new state government. He also talked about several new laws that he would be voting on soon and asked for the community's opinions. It was a real town hall meeting, with a lot of spirited discussion. One of the proposed laws has to do with limiting radio communications. The law would assign specific channels for emergency communications, and other channels as business lines. The law would eliminate, or regulate unnecessary communication by radio operators. The law also talks about licensing qualified radio operators.

Frank got up and read a statement that had been drafted by members of the Nuclear Survivors Radio Network. When Frank finished reading the collective opinion of NSRN, which was vehemently against the proposed radio law, he spoke his own mind. He said for the last six months the radio operators have been the ears of the survivors. Radio has been a constant link for all survivor groups. This law is a way of cutting off the link between survivors. It is a way of stopping the free flow of information. The members of NSRN believe this law to be a divide and conquer idea of the military and other groups outside of California. Everyday, fewer and fewer operators are heard outside of California.

Frank suggested that not only should this law be rejected but also the people of California should petition to have other radio operators, outside of California, allowed to broadcast openly and freely.

Frank's suggestion met with real approval and Teddy said he would raise the issue when he returns to Marysville. This morning dad and Teddy came to the school and gave a talk on our new state government and on the new federal government that is developing. Our new state capital is Marysville. Our new national capital seems to be Austin, Texas.

Both the state and national governments are made up of representatives. Each area of California sends a representative to Marysville. Soon each state, or section, of the country will send a representative to Texas. Each representative tells what his area has to offer as a resource. All the resources that an area can afford to share are collected and distributed evenly to all areas. The state has issued paper money called script. The military also has its own paper money called Military Payment Certificates (M.P.C.). People with certain skills, or in certain important jobs, are paid by either the state, or federal government, for their skill. Doctors don't bill people anymore, the government pays them. Engineers and laborers working for the state or military get paid in script or M.P.C.

The state has established stores in a number of the larger survivor centers like Marysville, Chico, Fort Bragg and Redding. The state has also developed mobile stores which drive to remote survivor areas and sell necessary goods. The federal government has started to put items in the state stores, but most of the provisions they provide are free.

All major industry that still exists, or has been started, is managed by the military. Individuals and groups all over the country have been encouraged to start small industries and businesses that are deemed essential.

Dad and Teddy explained to the students that our present government was an emergency government. Eventually the state and federal governments will stabilize and return to something more closely resembling our former government.

SEPTEMBER 17

I received a rather cryptic radio message from Major Lyle today. It said there were two people being assigned to New San Francisco (the name given to the area for the fishing plant near Stewart's Point) that I am supposed to meet with the next time I'm at the coast——Dr. Nancy Pagent, an oceanographer from Maine and Sgt. Lance Alcott, the Marine who will be in charge of security at the new construction site. I will have an opportunity to meet both tomorrow afternoon.

I have packed everything I need for a three month stay at the coast. Actually, I'm taking very little. I'm going there to work and learn about the ocean and the fish that live in it. I'm taking clothes, writing tablets, a jar of vitamin "C" that mom gave me, a guitar Frank gave me, and a small thirty-two automatic pistol dad gave me. Everything else I can get at the coast.

I will spend tonight with mom and dad and the girls. Tomorrow morning I will go with Sam to the boat and leave for the coast. I will miss my family and friends, but I am excited and anxious about going to the coast.

SEPTEMBER 19

I knew I was going to enjoy the coast, but I had no idea it would be as it is. Mrs. Foley is the sixty year old widow I am staying with. She is the perfect grandmother type. She was married for thirty years to a judge. He has been dead several years. Her sole delights are sipping sherry and gossiping about her neighbors. She is very slight of build with white hair, sparkling blue eyes and rosy cheeks. She reminds me of a little elf, or imp, because of her spry energy.

Besides Mrs. Foley being a real delight, I also met Lance. Sgt. Lance Alcott, Lance, met me when I came ashore from the fishing boat. He is twenty years old, blond, six feet tall, and has eyes the color of green Christmas trees. He is rather shy. When he helped me from the rowboat, he was kind of stammering about Major Lyle, and orders, and assignments. He was really cute when he realized he was making no sense and blushed bright red.

Lance and I talked last night after dinner. I told him the few things about me that Major Lyle had left out and he told me about himself.

He had been in the Marine Corps Reserves. When not training, he worked in a lumber camp in Idaho. He had been out marking trees when the bombs fell. The war came and went before he knew there had been a war. A forest ranger told him about it three days later. Lance spent two months in the mountains of Idaho helping organize the citizens and giving aid to survivors who straggled in from bombed out areas. When he heard the military was organizing in Nevada, he made his way there. His military identification card landed him a job as a military policeman. He was made a Sergeant and put in charge of security for buildings and storage areas. Major Lyle met him a week ago while inspecting a facility he was guarding. The major asked if he would be interested in heading security for the coast project. He was, and I'm glad.

Tomorrow I get to go to New San Francisco and the actual construction area. It's about six miles north of here. Giant helicopters, like the one Major Lyle let me ride in, have been ferrying in tons of equipment and building supplies to start the construction. Lance is in charge of guarding the materials.

SEPTEMBER 21

In school I remember reading and talking about California during the gold rush in 1849. San Francisco was a boom town with thousands of miners landing there on their way to the gold fields. New San Francisco must look much the same way. It's loud and raucous. Hundreds of men and women have pitched tents, or lean-tos, waiting to get jobs at the new construction site. There are some people who've come to set up businesses and make money off the many workers. There are tons of liquor being sold and traded. Some of it saved from the war, some of it recently made. There are parties, or celebrations, of one kind or another going on all the time.

I met Dr. Pagent today. She may be the one dark spot on my stay here. I introduced myself to the short, heavyset scientist. She gave me a quick glance, then returned to her notebook. She has the same studious air that Dr. Eller and Dr. Anderson had. It is as if she would rather have books and paper around her than people. When she finally took a break, she made sure to let me know my position. She told me if it were not for Major Lyle and other influential people, she would not have agreed to take on a student. Since I am here, I am to do exactly what she tells me. I am not to disturb her unless it is very important. She will give me one hour a day for questions.

Lance and I cut up on her all the way to Mrs. Foley's house. He drove me in the jeep the military assigned him. He is going to pick me up in the morning. Tomorrow work for me will begin in earnest.

SEPTEMBER 22

I am an official gopher. I go for this. I go for that. I go wherever, and whenever, Dr. Pagent sends me. She is setting up a lab on a cliff above the cove that will be the home of New San Francisco's fishing fleet. Right now the lab consists of four bare walls on a slab of cement, about the size of a two car garage. Dr. Pagent has tons of scientific equipment sitting in boxes outside the lab. She has me bring them in one at a time, unpack the contents and then wash all the tubes, beakers, vials, bottles and flasks she thinks are dirty. I'm getting dishpan hands, but I'm not getting much knowledge.

Tomorrow two workers will be assigned to help in setting

up the lab's equipment. Hopefully, that will allow me time to read the books Sam had Major Lyle send me. The books are all about the ocean and sea life. Whenever I find something I don't understand, I'm supposed to ask Dr. Pagent. Fat chance.

Lance brought Mrs. Foley into town today. He gave her a tour of where all the new buildings will be located. She was impressed with all the new people and new sources of available drinking sherry. She seems thrilled by all the activity.

Lance gave Mrs. Foley and I a ride home too. He stayed for dinner, but had to get back early, so we didn't have much time to talk.

SEPTEMBER 24

I blew up at Dr. Pagent today. I think I'm in trouble. I tried to ask a question while we were eating lunch. Actually, I was eating and Dr. Pagent was writing in her ridiculous notebook. The night before I had been reading about microscopic sea life. I asked Dr. Pagent how a diatom was different than an amoeba. She stopped writing, looked over at me, pondered my question for a few seconds, then said for me not to ask stupid questions. With that response she went back to her notebook. I sat staring at her little round head, bobbing up and down over that damned notebook, and I popped.

"Screw you! My question may be dumb, but your answer only shows how ignorant you are. You may be a genius about the ocean, but you don't know shit about people", I yelled at the top of her head.

To my surprise, she closed her notebook, got up from the packing box she had been sitting on, and headed for the lab, twenty feet away. Without looking at me, she said, "Let's get back to work."

We spent the afternoon setting up lab equipment on a

long work bench that had been brought in. I don't think we said ten words the whole time. At first I didn't care, then it got kind of spooky. I started thinking about what I had said to her and wondering if I had hurt her feelings.

When Lance came to take me to Mrs. Foley's, I was starting to really worry. I had visions of Dr. Pagent radioing dad, or Major Lyle, and telling them she wanted me out of her sight.

I plan to apologize tomorrow, if she'll listen. I think what she said to me sucked, but so did my reaction. I want to be here and learn, but the situation is frustrating. I will try to make it better tomorrow.

SEPTEMBER 25

Today was a great day. It started off a bit shaky, but it sure ended good. The rest of my time here at the coast is going to be wonderful.

I got to the lab at my regular time, about two hours after sunrise. As I approached the small building, my heart sank. Dr. Pagent was talking to Sam. My worst fear had happened, Dr. Pagent had radioed dad and he had sent Sam to get me. As I approached the two women, Sam saw me and came forward to give me a big hug. As we embraced I could see Dr. Pagent frowning.

"I didn't know you were acquainted with Jessie." Dr. Pagent said as she came towards us.

Sam explained that I was Gene Tineford's daughter and that I had been fishing and diving these waters for several months.

A rather dismayed look came over Dr. Pagent's face. She told both of us she was embarrassed. No one had told her that the girl who was going to be her student had any knowledge or background. If she had known of my experience and understanding, she would not have treated me so rudely. I wanted to say that she should have asked, but I decide she was being as gracious as she could and I didn't need to mess it up now. Instead, Dr. Pagent and I gave Sam a tour of our little laboratory. Dr. Pagent allowed me to explain what equipment we had set up and what tests we could conduct. Mostly I just repeated what Dr. Pagent had told me or others.

When we had finished our tour, Sam asked Dr. Pagent if the Scuba gear had arrived. My heart skipped a beat. Dr. Pagent pointed to an unopened box and said everything that had been ordered was on the manifest list. I went to the clipboard hanging on the wall and checked the list of equipment for box eighty-one. As I read, my excitement grew. Four Viking wet suits, four sets of twin seventy-two cubic inch tanks, four sets of Scuba Pro fins, four masks, regulators, gloves, booties, weights, belts, buoyancy compensators, gauges, everything we would need to dive.

"Air! What about air?" I asked, worrying that we would not be able to use the equipment. "How do we fill our tanks?"

Dr. Pagent smiled. It was the first time I could remember seeing her smile a wide, thin lipped smile across her chubby round face.

"Sgt. Alcott has a compressor stored in the military compound. We will have to fill the tanks there. The compressor, and the gas to run it have to be kept under guard." She told Sam and I.

"When can we go diving?" I asked the two women anxiously.

Sam explained that the lab had to be completed first. There was no sense in going sample collecting, if there was no place to test them.

Sam left after lunch to return to the fishing boats. I promised her that I would work hard to help Dr. Pagent complete the lab. I told her to give my family my love and to tell dad that I hope he will join us when we begin diving.

It was my father and my uncle Obie who had taught me to dive after my fourteenth birthday. I was certified through the Y.M.C.A. My dad and I enjoyed diving this coast together and had talked about diving all over the world. It will be great to be able to dive again.

I am resolved to getting the lab in shape as quickly as possible.

SEPTEMBER 27

Bill Newbury, Dave Winsby and I worked late last night finishing the fourth and final workbench in the laboratory. Bill and Dave are our two carpenter/workers. Bill is an older man and very competent at building things. He is short, bald, pink faced and very funny. He's always got something funny to say. Dave is quite a sight by himself. He stands about six four and weighs well over two hundred pounds. Bill is the brains and Dave is the brawn.

Dave once had kinky blond hair, now all he has is a patch of hair in the middle of his head. His face has some bad red scars and he appears to have a constant scowl. With the hair, the burn scars, and the scowl, he makes me think of a bleached out Mr. T. He's really quiet and nice, and he and Bill remind me of the two characters in Steinbeck's, Of Mice and Men.

When Dr. Pagent saw the work tables completed this morning, she smiled and spent the whole day setting up the lab equipment and work stations. By the time Lance came to pick me up, we had cleaned out the lab and removed all the empty crates. Dr. Pagent says we will soon be able to go specimen collecting.

SEPTEMBER 28

I did not go into the lab this morning. Dr. Pagent sent word that it was too cold for us to work. Lance drove to Mrs. Foley's to give me the message. He was in a foul mood and said the sudden cold that moved in last night was causing all kinds of problems at the settlement.

Sometime last night the temperature dropped twenty degrees. Thick fog has moved in along the coast. The air is frosty and the ground is icy. Lance said the temperature at the lab, at sunrise, was only twenty-five degrees. He told Mrs. Foley that he may have to take over some of her outbuildings to house workers. Apparently, the shanty houses that surround the settlement are not warm enough to protect the workers living there. The military is requesting that all local residents take in as many workers as possible. Large barracks buildings have been under construction for almost a month, but they are still not ready to be lived in.

I spent the afternoon cleaning out the extra bedroom in the main house and two of the outbuildings. I have suggested to Mrs. Foley that we ask Bill and Dave to move into one of the outbuildings. I told her they would be very handy to have around. She told me to invite them as soon as possible, so they could help repair the buildings here. I will ask them tomorrow if they would be interested in having a large house.

SEPTEMBER 30

The weather continues to be extremely cold. The temperature has remained right around thirty degrees. I went into the lab for a few hours yesterday and today, but it's too cold to work inside the small building. Dr. Pagent has ordered a small heater, of some sort, from the supply depot in Nevada. The settlement and the fish factory are a priority project for all the western states, so we get first choice on resources and materials. The military will fly in a heater as soon as possible. The cold front hit Nevada this morning. It is snowing there and nothing is flying.

Bill and Dave moved into one of the dusty old outbuildings

today. They came in from the settlement with Lance and I in Lance's jeep. They brought their bedrolls and some tools. You would have thought someone gave them the Taj Mahal, the way they acted when they saw the old run down guest house. I guess it is, to them. Lance says they've found adequate housing for all the workers who had come here looking for jobs. He says it's a tight fit, but at least no one will freeze to death. The new barracks will be finished soon. That will relieve the housing problem that now exists.

Tomorrow I'm going into the settlement to make a radio call to dad and mom. I'm sure the weather is a problem there, too. I also want to pick up a couple of books Dr. Pagent loaned me. She has certainly had a change of attitude since Sam's visit. She earnestly tries to help me understand the books and articles I've been reading. She can be very compassionate when she wants.

OCTOBER 1

Everything is at a standstill. It started snowing yesterday and hasn't stopped. The temperature is at zero and the snow is piling up fast. It is extremely bad news here if there is not a break in the weather soon. With no construction possible, the whole settlement is in grave danger. If the airstrip, worker's barracks and fish processing plant are not built soon, the project will fail and survival here could become brutal. Even with the ocean here, food is difficult to get in this kind of weather.

We need the airstrip completed to fly in food and building supplies. We need the barracks completed to make living conditions more tolerable. We also need to build the fish factory to feed this community and many others.

This morning there was a major conference on the radio. The radio here is at the military supply compound, next to the settlement. Dr. Pagent and I were summoned there by Lance. The radio conference call involved Jonah and Teddy in Marysville, dad, Frank, Donna and Sam at New Los Medanos, and our group at the coast.

Jonah and Teddy said they had been in contact with authorities in Nevada and Texas. They told us that weather satellites are still in place and working in outer space. The satellites show that the cold is going to continue for some time. However, the scientists believe there will be a break in the snow by next week. The military is going to attempt a major airlift of materials. Even though it involves working in the snow, the construction must take place.

The conference lasted for over an hour. Most of the talk centered around the airlift and the need to complete construction, but I also picked up a few cryptic phrases that I did not understand. The one phrase that most intrigued me was Jonah and Teddy asking dad about the progress of operation, "Ground Hog." He responded with a terse, "Everything proceeding as planned."

Lance has asked me to go around to all the local homes and communities and inform people of the upcoming airlift. There will be plenty of work for everyone, collecting and storing all the materials. Major construction work will begin, snow or not, as soon as the airlift is completed.

OCTOBER 2

I spent the entire day going from Ft. Ross to just north of Stewart's Point informing local residents and workers of the airlift and the rain-or-shine work edict. Workers are to report to the military compound tomorrow to be assigned specific duties during the airlift. Workers will also be polled to see if they have any specific skills.

Lance has asked Dr. Pagent, Mrs. Foley and me to help him assign workers to duty areas. We have to be at the supply compound at first light. Lance has issued us military long underwear, fur lined parkas, and snow boots. At least we'll be warmer than most of the people here.

I'm going to sleep early tonight. I am tired from all my travels today, and I have to be up early tomorrow.

OCTOBER 4

Yesterday was one of the longest days I can ever remember. From first daylight until long after darkness settled, we sat in the large tin quonset hut and planned for the airlift that will take place in three days. We assigned workers to jobs and areas. We listed the skills and backgrounds of a thousand cold and miserable workers. When the workers were all dealt with, we spent hours making up work crews of ten to twenty men and women. Each crew had at least one skilled carpenter, one heavy machine operator, and several manual laborers. Some crews had plumbers, others had electricians. To every tenth crew a building engineer was assigned. There are three major construction projects that have to be completed. The airstrip is number one. The barracks is number two, and the fish processing plant is three.

On the seventh of this month a continuous stream of large helicopters will unload supplies. While the helicopters are landing at the settlement, cargo transport planes will be parachute dropping additional supplies north of the settlement. Everything dropped, or unloaded, has to be stored in the supply compound, or at the appropriate construction site, before darkness falls.

OCTOBER 6

It has stopped snowing. The air is ice cold and thick, moist, fog covers the coast. Going anywhere is dangerous, the fog is so heavy. Visibility is about ten feet.

The weather conditions are keeping most everyone indoors. The result is tempers are starting to flair. Moods are somber and people are worried. I even yelled at Lance this morning when he made a remark about having to wait in his jeep while I got ready to go to the settlement. I snapped that he didn't have to come get me if he didn't want to. He just smiled and said it was the only part of the day he enjoyed and looked forward to. I felt really bad and I apologized as soon as we reached the lab.

Lance is a good person. I enjoy the time we spend together. I would like our relationship to be romantic, but
it isn't. We see each other everyday. We take walks together, or did, until the weather changed. We have long
discussions. We've even hugged and held hands a couple
of times, but not romantically. It is more like brother
and sister. I have not said anything to Lance about it.
I think it's because I fear the rejection I felt when Major
Lyle dismissed me like a child. Lance has never said anything, or given any indication, that we are anything other
than friends. Perhaps I am just a school girl to him too.
I guess I'll just wait and see.

Tomorrow is the big airlift. I will be very busy for the
next couple of days. When everything is a little less hectic,
I'm going to ask Lance how he feels about me. It may
be a bit forward, even improper, but in this day and age
I'm not sure what is proper.

OCTOBER 9

Landed and unloaded, one hundred and nine helicopter
flights. Recovered and stored, over four hundred supply
parachutes. Lost, one helicopter and crew and one full
parachute drop consisting of about twenty parachutes.
The helicopter touched down on a cliff near the ocean
and flipped over the ledge. The copter exploded when
it hit the rocks below. The parachute load came late
in the day, when the fog was thick. The plane must've
missed our drop zone signal. All of his chutes went into
the ocean. Some of the materials may be recovered by
small boats, but at this point, they're listed as lost.

Before I passed out from exhaustion this morning, I watched as the stored materials were inventoried. The amount
of supplies is staggering. There are small tractors, back-
hoes, steam shovels, and hand tools. There is pipe, corru-
gated tin sheets, pallets of bagged cement powder and
spools of electrical wire. There are bales of insulation
material and enough nails and screws to sink a barge.

That's just the building materials. We also received tons

of "C" ration cases, boxes of canned foods, boxes of pow-
dered milk, cooking utensils, tanks of propane, electrical
generators, and enough warm winter clothes to cover
everyone here, twice.

I'm sure work crews started building the airstrip and barracks today. I don't know. I sat down on a box in the
supply compound to rest and woke up a half day later
at Mrs. Foley's house.

The loss of human lives made the airlift very costly, but
it was ninety percent successful and will probably save
thousands of lives and this settlement. I will suggest
to Lance that some sort of memorial service be held for
the helicopter crew that perished. We should also send
a message of gratitude and sorrow to any friends, or family, they may have had.

Mrs. Foley's House

OCTOBER 10

Mrs. Foley refused to let me go to work today. She said
I've been doing too much lately and I need to rest. If
I don't rest, I'll get sick. I couldn't argue with her, I didn't
have the energy.

I spent all day writing letters to mom, dad, and Nellie.
I also ate a gallon of some wonderful soup Mrs. Foley
made. It was a kind of potato and clam chowder—thick
and rich. My stomach hurt from eating so much.

This afternoon I went out for a short walk to help digest my lunch. It is still cold and foggy and there is a lot of snow on the ground. I ran into Dave as I passed by his living quarters. He gave me a big toothless grin and a cheery wave, then he bumbled down the porch steps and came over to me.

"Hey, how ya feelin'? Better, huh? Boy. You was sure out of it. I carried ya in the house and you didn't budge. Feelin' better now, though, huh?"

Dave reminded me of a big St. Bernard, standing there rubbing his big gloved hands together and rocking from side to side. Smiling mindlessly, and hoping for some attention. I had an urge to reach out and pat him on the head, or scratch behind his ear. Instead, I asked him why he was home today. He told me Bill had made him stay home because he had worked for two straight days carrying supplies in from the snow.

He asked me if I wanted to sit on the porch and have some coffee. It was cold, but it beat being cooped up in the house. We sat on the porch on empty wooden boxes. He gave me a huge porcelain mug of hot, black coffee. I could feel the heat of the cup through my gloves and it warmed me.

Dave talked aimlessly for about ten minutes, almost non-stop. I listened, and nodded when I thought it appropriate. All of a sudden he stopped. He looked around as if he just realized where he was. He looked at me rather sheepishly and spoke in a much clearer and articulate voice.

"Wow! I must have really been babbling along. I'm sorry. I guess I do that on occasion. Bill never tells me to shut up. I think he enjoys my chatter. We'd both better get inside. We've had enough fresh air for today."

With an embarrassed look on his big face, he took my coffee cup and went inside the little house. I waited a moment to see if he was coming back out. When he didn't, I got up and walked back to the main house. Dave's sudden change of demeanor really startled me.

OCTOBER 11

It is still not snowing, but it is sure cold. The scenery is spectacular. I am awed by the beauty of snow in the trees and on the cliff ledges above the ocean. The fog hanging just above the tree tops and blurring the horizon adds an eerie surrealism to everything.

The mood at the settlement is no longer gray and somber. The airlift lifted spirits, as well as supplies. With construction work well in progress, everyone has a purpose, an objective. There is no time for feeling down or sad.

I went to the lab and got a real shock. I walked in and the heat hit me like a blast furnace. A small wood burning stove at one end of the room was keeping the place at about seventy-five degrees. Dr. Pagent was sitting at one of the work benches with Bill. They were sitting on tall wooden stools that Bill had made. As I started removing all my warm weather gear, Bill came forward with a large cup of hot chocolate. I could smell the chocolate clear across the room. I suddenly flashed on the last time I had smelled that aroma. It was last Christmas morning—an eternity ago.

We all sat around the stove and drank hot chocolate. Dr. Pagent told me she had laid out the major experiments we needed to perform. All we need now are some specimens to test. She told me she had contacted Samantha regarding a diving trip to collect the specimens we would need. Sam, dad and Jerry are going to try and make the trip day after tomorrow. If the weather holds, they will be here early in the morning to fish and dive. I am excited.

I spent the afternoon making a list of items to look for while underwater. Dr. Pagent and I are going to go tide pool hunting tomorrow. We need specimens from both sources.

OCTOBER 12

Today was a very relaxing day. Dr. Pagent and I spent

all morning and a part of this afternoon walking the beaches, rocks and ledges of a six mile stretch of coast. We dug in sand, looked under rocks and hunted in tidepools. There is very little snow close to the water. It has all melted, or been washed away.

I probably learned more about shoreline sea life today than in all the reading I've ever done. Dr. Pagent is a true genius in her field. She's like a walking library, constantly giving out information. I can understand why she was chosen for this job.

Lance is coming by this evening for dinner. Mrs. Foley invited him to join Dave, Bill and I. It will be the first time in awhile that Lance and I have been able to just sit and talk. Even if I do most of the talking.

If all goes well with the weather, the fishing boats will be here early in the morning. Tomorrow I may get an opportunity to do some diving. It would be my first time scuba diving since August of last year. I'm sure it will be a thrill for dad, too. He really loves the ocean and always enjoyed his dive trips.

OCTOBER 14

Yesterday was the best day I can remember since the war. Dad, Sam and Jerry showed up shortly after first light. They came on Survivor I. The other fishing boat stayed farther south to fish and return to New Los Medanos.

We all had a brief meeting at the lab to discuss where we would go and what we were looking for. After an hour of discussion, we loaded the fishing boat and headed out to sea. About a quarter mile out we anchored on the ocean side of a reef.

Dad, Sam and I suited up in the rubbery skins that would keep us dry and warm underwater. I was fully dressed and checking my gear when I realized that Dr. Pagent was not suiting up. I went over and asked her why she wasn't diving. She gave me a very cool look and said she wouldn't be diving today. It was the same cold calm voice she had used the day I blew up at her. After she spoke, she took out her notebook and went inside the boat's wheelhouse. I stood there rather dumbfounded and stared after her. Sam's hand on my shoulder broke the reverie.

"Dr. Pagent has contracted a disease from radioactivity. She can never dive again. It makes her very upset. She is very envious that you can dive and she can't." Sam told me as we moved to the back of the boat and prepared to enter the water.

Jerry had built a dive platform on the back of the boat and cut a passageway through the fantail wall. He removed the wooden gate and we all stepped onto the platform. The ocean was calm. There was no wind and only gently rolling swells.

A last minute check of each other's gear and we splashed into the ocean. I floated head and shoulders out of the water and waited for the first rush of cold water into my wetsuit. It took a moment for me to realize there would be no such rush because I was wearing a dry suit. Only my hands and face felt the bite of the icy salt water.

I adjusted my face mask, cleared my regulator and waited for the thumbs up sign to begin my descent. Dad made an adjustment of the compass on his wrist and gave Sam and I the signal to dive. I put my face down in the water and located the anchor line. I executed a jackknife maneuver, gave a big dolphin kick and slid quickly into the depths. Twenty feet down, I caught hold of the anchor line and righted myself. I squeezed my nose and cleared my ears and waited for Sam and dad to lead the way.

Dad pointed to the top of the reef fifteen feet below and headed out. Sam followed and I brought up the rear. The visibility struck me right away. In the past I remembered the visibility on a normal day being eight to ten feet and cloudy. On a good day I had seen twenty feet and hazy. Today it was forty feet and clear. It was spectacular! I stopped at the top of the reef to once again squeeze my nose and equalize the pressure in my ears. As I did, I looked up and watched as my silvery air bubbles danced and undulated to the surface, thirty-five feet above.

Dad and Sam slid down the side of the reef, trailing hundreds of expanding bubbles that raced for the surface. I unhooked the webbed nylon goody bag from my weight belt and began to search the nooks and crevices of the reef for the specimens we needed. At fifty feet I came across a huge white sea anemone. It stood like a giant sea flower in full bloom. It was two feet high, a foot thick and had six inch long tentacles branching out from its center. Around its base were a half dozen smaller anemones. In the light, the cluster looked like a large diamond surrounded by bagets. I wished I had a camera.

Scuba Diving For Specimens

My dive lasted almost thirty-five minutes. I finished with almost three hundred pounds of air pressure in my tank. Not bad for not having dove in over a year. The average depth had been fifty feet, with my deepest descent to sixty. I had caught up to Sam and dad when they had started back to the boat. I joined them and we ascended the anchor line together.

At the surface Jerry and Dr. Pagent took our specimen filled goody bags from us, then helped us onto the dive platform. As we removed our gear we handed it to the crew members on board who seemed as excited as we were. Everyone was talking and asking us questions. As I pulled off my weight belt and stepped onto the deck, I looked for Dr. Pagent. She was on the aft side of the boat looking into one of the goody bags. I walked over to her and stood next to where she was kneeling.

"I hope we got everything we went after," I said leaning down to her.

"It looks marvelous, Jessie," she responded as she stood up.

To me she looked like she felt miserable. I stepped closer and gave her a hug.

"I'm sorry. It was beautiful. I wish you could have been down there with me." I said softly into her ear.

"I was. I really was there. In spirit," she said smilingly, as we pulled apart. "Thank you for thinking of me."

The day ended when we placed all our specimens in large salt water tanks at the lab. It had been an exciting and successful experience. Dad and Sam spent the night and went back early this morning.

OCTOBER 15

It started snowing again this morning. It was almost as if nature said, "Okay, I'll give you a few more days to get yourselves together, but that's all." We are all warm and living and working comfortably now. The new barracks will be completed by next week. That will relax the housing problem. Now it is just a matter of building an airstrip and the fish processing plant.

Dr. Pagent and I have been in the lab all of yesterday afternoon and today. She is giving me on-the-job training. She has me set up each experiment, explains what the test is designed for and tells me what results we are looking for. So far she hasn't touched one apparatus, or one specimen. She has me doing it all and is merely acting as supervisor and teacher. I am learning the names of equipment, scientific terminology and the proper Latin names of all our specimens; species, genus and family.

Water and seaweed samples taken by Dr. Pagent and the boat crew, while we were diving, are also being tested. We are trying to determine how much radioactivity has entered the ocean, how much is being absorbed by plant and animal life, and if tides and currents are increasing, or decreasing the radioactive levels.

Some of the experiments get immediate results. Some experiments can last weeks. Many of the tests need to be done over and over to detect subtle changes. The testing will be going on long after I have returned to New Los Medanos.

I feel I have gained a real friend in Dr. Pagent. Originally, I was just a worker, like Dave or Bill. Then I became a student, learning from a teacher. Now, I'm a student worker, but my teacher and boss is my good friend. We laugh now and talk. I'm starting to learn about my friend.

Dr. Pagent, like dad, is dying. Not as rapidly, but perhaps more cruelly. She has a cancerous disease that is eating up all the calcium in her body. It attacks her teeth, her bones, her fingernails, and her already thin hair. Eventually, her bones will not support her body. She will become bedridden, and, if she lives longer, she will be crushed by her own weight. She has decided she will not let her illness go that far. I have to agree with her feelings.

OCTOBER 17

I got a real surprise yesterday. Lance came by in the morning and picked me up as usual. We drove into the settlement, but instead of going to the lab we went to the military compound, where a small helicopter was waiting. On board, and waiting, were Dr. Pagent, Jonah and Teddy.

The copter flew over New Los Medanos and the mines in the hills above the community. I could see large windmills erected on the hilltops above the mines. We landed long enough to say hello to dad and mom, then picked up Donna and Dr. Bronson and headed towards Marysville.

When we landed at the new capital I was somewhat surprised. Even with snow covering almost everything I could still see the enormous amount of construction going on. Many large underground buildings were being built. The building in town that had been city hall before the war, and the state capital since, had been substantially enlarged. Radiating out from the capital building were eight long, low structures, each as long and wide as a football field.

The activity around the city reminded me of a gold rush boomtown, the same as the coast settlement. Everyone in Marysville was dressed in the grey-green fatigues that have become the unisex uniforms of post war America. Warm, comfortable, durable, and as sexless as you could get. It is often difficult to tell men from women, since hairstyles or the lack of, are all the same.

We attended a meeting of several state legislators, a group of military men and women, and two government representatives from Texas. The entire meeting was a presentation by various members of the state government and local scientists, especially Dr. Pagent. Reports were given on specific construction projects around the northern part of the state, the expected completion date of the project at the coast, and the physical and mental health of California survivors.

I was interested in the building projects, but much more interested in the final topic regarding the survivors. Donna gave the report on this subject. She explained how a listing of all known survivors had been developed and the efforts made to relocate all survivors to existing communities. She spoke of the general health of survivors, from colds to major diseases. She told the two men from Texas that medical testing was being completed on all survivors and that each survivor was being ranked in one of three categories: Category "A" is a survivor who has little to no radiation effects and is in good to excellent health; "B" is a person who has had major radiation exposure, but is in good health; "C" is everyone who has been exposed to large amounts of radiation and is in poor to fair health. Donna further explained that with the exception of herself, Dr. Bronson and Dr. Pagent, everyone at the meeting was in category "A".

The two men from Texas asked a lot of questions of each person giving a report. Several times during the meeting the term "Operation Groundhog" came up, but it was never directly discussed. I made a mental note to ask Dr. Pagent and Dr. Bronson what the term referred to.

OCTOBER 18

Since the war I have experienced a great range of emotions. I've had high highs and low lows. I've been happy, sad, angry, scared, excited, bored, lonely, frustrated and a few states of mind I can't even name. This evening I'm experiencing a feeling I can only describe as sad awe.

It was cold and windy this morning, but not snowing. Bill, Dave and I walked into the settlement from Mrs. Foley's. Dave was his usual talkative self. He made commentary on everything we saw on our early morning trek. His voice was that same punch drunk slur that I have become accustomed to hearing. On reaching the lab each of us began regular tasks. I resumed the draining and filling of salt water tanks inside the lab. Bill set about measuring wall space for new shelves. Dave was outside sawing planks of wood that Bill had measured and marked previously.

The explosion occurred only an hour after we had begun

work. Though the blast was over a quarter of a mile away, it rocked the lab and rattled all the equipment inside. As the major blast rumbled through the small room, I could hear smaller, less powerful explosions going off.

Bill yelled for me to stay put and ran outside. Visions of Lance, Dr. Pagent, and others raced through my mind and I took off after Bill. As soon as I exited the door I could see the orange flame ball and the thick black smoke above the snow covered trees. Small, deep thuds punctuated the growl of the initial fire and explosion. The second thing I noticed upon exiting the lab was Dave sprinting down the road towards the fire. Bill was standing at the edge of the road yelling after Dave.

I ran up next to Bill and watched Dave disappear around the bend in the road leading to the airstrip construction site. Bill turned to me with tears in his eyes and desperation on his face. His voice was shrill when he spoke.

"We have to stop him! He'll be hurt! He'll go crazy around that fire." Bill's words shot out above the roar of the fire.

I grabbed Bill's arm and started down the road towards the disaster. At first, he seemed to hesitate, but soon he was trotting along beside me. The closer we got to the fire the hotter the air became. When we rounded the bend the severity of the explosion and fire became real. Against the hillside, away from the ocean, the workers had stored hundreds of barrels of gasoline. The gas stored here was for the small tractors and graders working on the airstrip. The bulk of the gasoline had exploded and individual barrels were still overheating and blowing up. Some of the fifty gallon drums just took off like rockets, shooting into the air and trailing smoke behind them. There was chaos and confusion everywhere. People were running all over the area. There was shouting and screaming. Two houses nearby were in flames, a completed portion of the airstrip was blown away, and trees knocked down by the explosion were burning.

In the midst of all this craziness I saw Dave, not the stumbly, fumbly Dave I normally encountered, but the Dave I had seen that day on the porch drinking coffee. He was standing in the middle of the partially constructed, partially ruined, airstrip. He was grabbing frantically running workers and directing them to various areas. He was organizing first aid and fire fighting efforts. I watched as he led a half dozen men close to the explosion site and helped remove the bodies of injured workers.

When two tanker trucks full of seawater reached the site, I jumped at the chance to help. Bill and I attached a pump to the opening on one of the truck's tanks and began spraying a stream of water at smaller fires around the main fire's perimeter. As the water trucks moved around the airstrip area, the situation began to calm down. There was less chaos and more organization. Soldiers from the military compound, workers from other sites and local citizens showed up to help out. Major effort went into putting out smaller fires, evacuating injured and keeping the main fire from doing further damage to the airstrip construction.

Bill and I worked from the top of a water truck for over an hour. The whole time Bill kept a frantic lookout for Dave. He kept telling me he hoped Dave would be all right. When we were finally relieved by two soldiers, Bill immediately headed to where he had last seen Dave. Near the main fire Dave was still directing workers. He had organized small work groups to remove all debris from near the fire. They had cleared a hundred yard break on three sides of the fire. The fourth side was a steep wall of a rocky hill.

Bill and I went to where Dave stood talking to one of the military engineers. Bill gently placed his hand on Dave's shoulder. Dave turned to Bill, his face was covered with soot and streaked by sweat. He gave Bill a big smile and went back to talking to the engineer. Bill and I moved off several yards to be out of the worker's way.

"Bill, how come Dave does these Jekyll and Hyde routines? I saw him go through this change once before." I asked Bill as he watched Dave closely.

"Dave was a police officer for about ten years. A really intelligent young man. He had citations for bravery, commendations, awards. He was a genuine hero. When the war started he helped direct evacuation and shelter efforts. He barely made it to cover before the missiles hit. Almost as soon as the exploxions stopped, he was out setting up relief and aid stations. He got burned from running into a burning house to rescue a woman and child. Later he found out that his own wife and children had been killed by missile warheads. The shock and realization of his own loss was too much for him. His mind snapped.

When I found him, he was sitting on a bombed out street corner giving away what little food he had to kids scavenging in the streets. His mind is like a ten year old's, but every so often his mind clicks on and he's his old self. Problem is, you never know when it will turn on and off. It could get him killed." Bill told me the story without ever taking his gaze from Dave.

A few minutes later Dave came over to us. He said they were going to let the fire burn itself out and there was nothing more we could do. He told Bill he was tired and was going back to the lab and take a nap.

We all walked in silence the four or five hundred yards to the laboratory. At the lab we found Dr. Pagent and Lance. They had been down south since early this morning and had just returned a short while ago. They told us they had been worried about us when they first returned, but had been informed we were all fine. The entire group went inside to get warm. I watched as Dave curled up on the floor next to the stove and fell asleep.

Lance had gone and returned. Bill had finished measuring the shelf space and Dr. Pagent and I had finished our chores by the time Dave woke up. It was the child minded Dave that stretched and yawned by the warm stove. He had no recollection of the fire or his efforts in fighting it. He was a little upset that he had fallen asleep and was dirty.

Lance drove Bill and Dave back to their living quarters.

It was a truly amazing day.

OCTOBER 20

The gasoline fire is still burning. It is not the inferno it was. There is black smoke and small flames, but it continues to burn.

Construction is continuing on the airstrip, but there is concern that it cannot be finished without fuel for the heavy equipment. Lance has radioed in a report on the fire and the loss of almost two-thirds of our fuel supply. He also reported the death of two workers, the severe burns on three more workers, and the injury of ten more. His report ended with an explanation of how gasoline, leaking from damaged containers, had pooled under the wooden pallets and had ignited when a forklift truck had gone into the storage area.

Dave is oblivious to his own heroics. He keeps asking Bill if they can walk down and see where the smoke's coming from. It is sad that such a good person is afflicted so. Maybe it's more merciful than constantly being aware of his personal loss. Dave doesn't understand why workers throughout the settlement keep stopping by the lab and saying thank you to him.

OCTOBER 21

It is really snowing heavily. Some construction work above ground has been halted, but underground work and work inside makeshift shelters continues.

Most of my day at the lab was spent reading. There is little for me to do right now. Dr. Pagent has been giving me oral quizzes on names and characteristics of local fish. It's hard, but it's fun and I learn a lot.

This evening I'm supposed to go with Lance to the radio

shack at the military compound. I want to make a call to New Los Medanos and we are just going to sit and listen to the radio chatter. I have not done that in awhile and I miss it.

OCTOBER 22

I was a bit upset by my call to New Los Medanos last night! I spoke to Frank for a short while, until dad came to the microphone. Frank says everything is fine. He said I wouldn't recognize the place, it's so clean. The weather hasn't been a major factor there, except for the fishing boats. He told me mom and the girls were fine, but then he added that dad looks really bad. I began to question him for saying it, but got cut short when dad came on the air. Dad's picture of everything was rosy and corresponded with what Frank had said. I asked how he was and how he was feeling. He gave me his, never felt better, routine. I wasn't sure if it was radio interference, a quaver in dad's voice, or what Frank had said, but I didn't feel that dad was honest about his health.

I had wanted to talk to Nellie about what she was doing with the little kids for Halloween, but she did not come to the radio. I talked as long as I could, then we all said good-bye.

On the ride back to Mrs. Foley's, I told Lance I wanted to go down to New Los Medanos for a visit. I told him I had an uneasy feeling about my dad. He said he'd see what he could do.

OCTOBER 23

It is still snowing heavily. Getting around is becoming a bit difficult. Dr. Pagent has said if it is snowing to-morrow morning, not to come to work.

Lance wound up staying here last night because the road

was so bad. He slept in front of the fireplace. He went into the settlement early, so Bill and I walked in. Dave stayed with Mrs. Foley to give her a hand.

Even with the lab stove working overtime the little room never got comfortably warm. Every time the door opened all the heat would rush out. Lance came by around lunch time and said some of the workers had gotten frost bite and a couple were suffering from mild hypothermia. I'm not sure what the temperature is, but it is cold. Lance says more construction will be stopped if the thermometer continues to drop.

OCTOBER 24

I cannot remember the last time I felt boredom. It has been a long time, I'm sure. Today I tried anything and everything to shake off the frustration of non-accomplishment. I helped Mrs. Foley make sugar cookies for Dave. I made up a Fairy Godmother costume for Halloween. I used an old wedding dress of Mrs. Foley's. I wrote mom and dad a long letter about my experiences here at the coast. I finally resorted to writing this entry in my diary, even though there is nothing to say.

Bored!!! Bored, bored, bored. I would rather be back in the coal mines than sitting here doing nothing. At least in the mines there was always something to do. Even working would make time go faster.

I hope Lance makes it by later. He is not a great conversationalist, but it's better than sitting here talking to the walls.

OCTOBER 26

It stopped snowing yesterday afternoon. The whole area looks like the inside of a giant freezer. The snow is thick and powdery. A small tractor went down the highway and cleared the snow early this morning.

I walked into the settlement with Bill and Dave, but Dr. Pagent told me to report to Lance at the military compound. I walked over to the office where Lance is headquartered. He was in a great mood. He was running around the little office and joking with soldiers who work as clerks.

As soon as I arrived he buckled up in his heavy coat and we went out to his jeep. He drove me back to Mrs. Foley's and told me to pack an overnight bag. He explained that several helicopters were coming in to resupply gasoline lost in the fire. After their delivery he was going to have one of them drop me off at New Los Medanos.

I packed clothes, some books and my Halloween costume. We returned to the settlement and I stopped to tell Dr. Pagent I would be gone for a few days. I gave Bill and Dave hugs and told them I'd see them soon.

I waited for an hour, before five huge transport helicopters landed and started unloading barrels of fuel and miscellaneous boxes. When the unloading was complete, Lance ushered me onto one of the copters. He gave me a kiss on the cheek and said he'd see me in a few days.

The helicopter lifted off in a flurry of blown snow. The trip only lasted a short while. We flew directly to New Los Medanos over a landscape of white. The cover of snow was broken only by the lines of streams, creeks, or rivers. When we reached New Los Medanos I was surprised. A great deal of construction has taken place in the short time I have been at the coast. There is a new building in the area that used to be the front parking lot. The whole place is covered with snow and ice and looks like a giant ice castle.

Mom and the girls were really happy to see me. I spent a little time with mom while I unpacked, but I spent the whole afternoon at the schoolroom in the college cafeteria. I told Nellie and the kids all about the coast and the work going on there. I told them about diving in the ocean and showed them pictures in books to help them understand. Everyone was interested and enthusiastic. They asked a lot of questions. I enjoy sharing what I've learned and experienced.

Dad is up at the mines and won't be back until tomorrow. The snow is too thick to make the trip up, so I'll wait for him.

OCTOBER 27

I had an opportunity to get around and visit with people I haven't seen for awhile. Frank and I talked for quite a spell. He says he will be moving up to the mines soon on a permanent basis. He says they have built a complete communications center there. He told me it has a huge radio tower and even a microwave dish.

I got a chance to talk with Sam and Jerry when they came up from the fishing boats. They said they were going to attempt a fishing trip in a few days. That will be my ride back to the coast settlement. Sam told me they are building a storage area for the boats and living quarters for the fishing crews down at the river. She said the fishing group spends most of its time there anyway.

Dr. Bronson and Donna were both busy with chores, but they took time to ask about the coast and tell me what they had been doing. Both of them talked about new projects they were involved with, including work at the mines. I had just started to question Donna about the mines when Nellie came in and said dad was in the living quarters changing and wanted to see me. I told Dr. Bronson and Donna I'd talk to them later and left with Nellie.

The shock of seeing my father made me cry. I'm sure he thought I was crying because we hadn't seen each other in a while, and I tried to smile through my tears. When I hugged my father I was afraid I would break the frail body I held. He has lost a great deal of weight and his skin is pale and gaunt. He looks twenty years older than he is. He moves slowly, stiffly and looks weak.

Mom, Nellie, Jamie and Jackie sat and listened as I told dad about my adventures and experiences at the coast. We talked until dinner time. Dad took the girls and headed for the cafeteria for the evening meal. I stayed back with mom under the pretext of changing clothes. When dad left the cubicle I spoke to mom. I asked her how dad's health had declined so rapidly. She told me it was almost overnight. He is getting weaker and weaker and Dr. Frantz says he may not live out the year.

Mom said one of the problems is that dad won't slow down, or rest. He is constantly working. He spends the majority of his time at the mines. Mom says making the mines into an underground city is an obsession with dad. We continued to talk while we walked to the cafeteria of the college. Mom is certain that dad is intentionally working hard, avoiding rest and ignoring medical attention. She feels that dad doesn't want to be a burden and he doesn't want to linger, or suffer.

At the cafeteria I saw many familiar faces and a few new ones. Many of the community's inhabitants are staying at the mines construction project. I was also pleased to see several pregnant women. Apparently not all survivors are afraid to attempt having children. Hopefully, healthy babies will be born again.

OCTOBER 29

Yesterday I spent the day helping Nellie and Shellie at the school. I am really impressed with the progress Shellie has made. When we first saw her she was like a zombie. Now she is talkative, smiling, and infinitely helpful. She can't stop trying to do things for others. Nellie says that Shellie and Frank spend a lot of time together. That would be nice. Frank has been lonely ever since Emil was killed by the roaches.

When dad returned to the mines, I went with him. We rode up in a jeep powered by alcohol. The ride took about twenty minutes. Even with slushy snow on the ground, it was faster than the walk I used to remember.

The main entrance to the mine complex is the same entrance we had used almost eleven months earlier to escape the war. Now, it is a large opening with a metal door. The passageway has been enlarged, so that a good size tractor could travel through it.

The inside of the complex no longer resembles a network of mines. It is like being inside a large building. The tunnels are hallways, with sandstone walls. Large caverns are storage areas, or manufacturing shops. There are areas set up like small apartment cubicles. The entire complex has a unique lighting system. The electricity is supplied by generators deep inside. Wind and steam are the main fuel sources.

I spent the day with dad. He showed me all of the innovations he had added since my last visit.

On our ride back to the college I asked dad about his health. He started off, in his cheery voice, about being fine, but he stopped when he saw my face getting angry and red. He pulled the jeep to a halt about a mile from the college. He sat quietly, staring at the steering wheel. After a few moments he turned and smiled a sheepish grin.

"I never could buffalo you. Even when you were little." He said impishly. Then he sobered. "I'm dying. I lived through a nuclear war, just to dry up and wither away. I'm angry. I've enjoyed the challenge of survival. My only regret up to now is that you and your sisters have had to lose everything and experience the horrors of war. When we were in the mines, after the missiles hit, I resolved that I would come out fighting. I would be a leader. Now I will probably never see the results of my work." His voice trailed off and he got quiet again. After a few moments he smiled and patted me on the knee.

"When I first started feeling the effects of this disease, I decided I was going to use all my time and energy finishing the projects I've started. I refuse to rest and the medicine they gave me makes me too drugged to work. Rest and medicine will only prolong the inevitable for a few months at best. I would rather accomplish what I have started. When I'm gone I want people to remember me for what I've done, not how I died. Does that make sense?" He asked when he was finished.

"It makes all the sense in the world." I told him, as tears welled up in my eyes. Millions of people have died. Most of the people I knew before the war are dead. I have seen great pain and suffering that turned my stomach. Nothing I have seen, or experienced, prepares me for the coming death of my father.

OCTOBER 30

Shellie, Nellie and I spent the whole day preparing the school kids for Halloween. First, we had all of the kids make decorations to hang everywhere. When the cut-outs of black cats, pumpkins, ghosts and witches had been finished and hung throughout the community, we started decorating the kids. Using old clothes, props and paints, we created hoboes, clowns, Raggedy Anns and Andys, a couple of angels, and some space aliens. None of the kids wanted to be ghosts, monsters, or skeletons. I guess they've all seen enough scary sights.

OCTOBER 31

Shortly after the evening meal, a party was held in the cafeteria. There were some simple cakes and candies for all the kids. Parents and other adults came to watch the costume contest. I dressed in my Fairy Godmother outfit and acted as Master of Ceremonies for the contest. We gave a blue ribbon to every kid who participated. To the three kids who were voted best costumes, we gave a book, as a prize.

Shellie, Nellie, and Donna gave me a special prize for

helping out. All the kids, with Donna's help, had made a huge quilt for me. Kids had donated scraps of material and put their names on them. The scraps were sewn together and filled with some type of insulating material. The quilt is thick and warm.

The adults and kids had a good time. Everyone left in a good mood. It may not have been as festive as previous Halloweens, but it was another positive remnant of society pulled from the ashes of war.

NOVEMBER 1

Tomorrow I will be returning to the coast. Sam is taking one of the fishing boats out early in the morning. She will drop me off before they start fishing.

When I originally went to the coast, I had been excited. I had fought and argued to be allowed to go. My excitement and determination had masked my other feelings. Tonight I have an emptiness inside. I am torn between wanting to be here with my family and wanting to be at the coast learning and helping. I want to be an adult and go out into the real world. I also want to be a child and play and have others look after me and worry for me. I don't like having responsibilities and working, but I do. Maybe I wouldn't feel this way if I were older. Maybe I wouldn't feel this way if it weren't for dad's illness. Perhaps this is what everyone feels when it is time to leave home.

NOVEMBER 3

It started snowing shortly after the fishing boat left New Los Medanos. Sam was worried that she wouldn't be able to make it back if she waited too long. She dropped me off several miles south of the settlement and headed back to a safe harbor. I trekked through the gently falling snow to Mrs. Foley's house.

I sat by the fireplace until late last night. I told Mrs.

Foley about my trip and the Halloween celebration. I recounted the story for Bill and Dave, and later in the evening for Lance. No one here had celebrated. It was considered too childish by some and completely forgotten by others. Most people have lost track of time. They have no concept of what day or month it is.

This morning I went to work at the lab and had Dr. Pagent in tears, laughing as I described the costumes the kids had worn. She has never had children, but she says she loves kids. She told me she used to do volunteer work at Christmas time, working for an orphanage. She would probably be a good mother. She will never know.

NOVEMBER 4

It is work as usual. Most of the simple experiments have been completed at the lab. Now it is a matter of writing test results and observing long range and ongoing experiments.

So far, we have determined that radiation levels in the ocean are far lower than expected. That some forms of sea life absorb more radiation than others. That some fish can purge radioactivity from their bodies. That the photosynthesis process has been greatly reduced due to the lower levels of ultraviolet light reaching the Earth's surface. It doesn't seem like much knowledge for all the time and effort put in.

NOVEMBER 7

It isn't snowing, but the temperature is really down. There is also a thick fog hanging wetly along the coast. It is so cold that it burns your nostrils when you breathe.

A truck convoy left here today for Marysville. It is carrying a load of frozen fish and Dr. Pagent's report on the Pacific Ocean and its sea life. I am listed on the report as a coauthor, along with Sam. I feel a lot of pride at having been a participant in so important a project. Several million people will be fed by the seafood harvested and processed here.

If construction continues without interruption, the fish plant and the airstrip will be operational after the new year. Tons of processed fish can be shipped out of here every week.

Lance and I are planning a little celebration for Dr. Pagent. It will be for a small group of friends.

NOVEMBER 9

It is chaotic here. Everyone is in a panic. Several people are dead. Many have been injured. Most of the deaths and injuries occurred on construction sites. One woman was killed when her house slipped into the ocean. Several men were hurt by a landslide near the main road.

A major earthquake hit California yesterday. I was in about thirty feet of water when the earth started moving. I wasn't aware of the earthquake on land. I was aware of rocks tumbling around and the movement of the ocean changing, but it was not dramatic. Something inside me said a mild earthquake underwater would be a big quake on land. I surfaced immediately. Lance was on the rocky shore, waving frantically. I swam ashore and crawled out onto the rocks. Lance asked me if I felt the quake. I told him I had, but that it seemed mild.

At that moment, a second shock forced me to my knees. Rocks from the hillside above rolled down and splashed into the water. Before the temblor had stopped, Lance was headed for his jeep.

We drove to the settlement over slush covered ground. When we arrived, we could see the damage and hear the chaos. Still dressed in my diving suit, I ran for the lab. Lance drove to the military compound.

At the lab I found Dave and Bill comforting a near hysterical Dr. Pagent. She was not hurt, but the quakes had scared her badly. Inside the small building, everything was smashed. All the glass equipment lay shattered on the floor. Our little heater stove was sitting awkwardly off its foundation.

Dave and Bill took Dr. Pagent and went to check on Mrs. Foley. I told them I would be along as soon as I could. They went south and I went north, to the military compound. When I got there, I found Lance breaking his men up into two groups. One group was to lead search and rescue operations, the other group was to calm the people and maintain order. I went with the first group. Several soldiers and myself went to some of the more remote homesteads to check on the conditions of the buildings and people.

By early this morning most of the dead and injured were accounted for and all major damage has been assessed.

NOVEMBER 11

We have had several aftershocks over the last two days. We have no way of judging the magnitude of the temblors, but they are strong. Strong enough to cause minor damage.

I have been staying close to the radio shack at the military compound. The radio has been in constant contact with all the communities in northern California. Each area has reported its damage and death toll. The north coast has been the hardest hit. Crescent City and Fort Bragg have both reported major damage and loss of life. The only community that has not made radio contact is New Los Medanos.

Lance spoke briefly with Teddy in Marysville. Teddy says there is some damage there, but no loss of life. Teddy told Lance he is requesting a helicopter to fly over New Los Medanos as soon as the weather permits. I am getting anxious.

NOVEMBER 12

Lance came by Mrs. Foley's this morning. He looked very
bleak as he told me there had been a message from New
Los Medanos. The message was sent to Marysville and
intercepted by the radio operator here. I knew the information was bad when Lance came over and hugged me.

"It was a short, garbled, radio transmission." Lance said
into my ear. He stepped back and took a slip of paper
from his jacket pocket. "Hundreds dead. Living quarters
and main college structure collapsed. Survivors moving
to mines. Instituting Groundhog. Will report again when
radio equipment completely functional." Lance read aloud
to Bill, Dave, Mrs. Foley, and I.

The shock was too great for me to react emotionally,
this morning. A thousand questions raced through my
mind, but only one thought surfaced and stayed. I have
to go home. Now!!!

It is late in the afternoon here. I am going to walk into
the settlement and ask Lance to make arrangements for
me to get home.

NOVEMBER 13

I am packing gear for a quick march to New Los Medanos.
Lance cannot arrange transportation, because of the
weather. There has been no news coming from home.
I will walk from here to San Francisco Bay and then try
to find a way across to the other side.

LATER

Dr. Pagent and Lance came by awhile ago. Lance has
spoken with Frank. Frank is alive and finishing construction of the radio transmitter at the mines. Dad asked
Frank to contact me. Dad wants me to come home right

away. He says the fishing boat cannot get out of San Francisco Bay right now. The earthquake turned the Bay Area into a giant mudhole and made it impassable at the mouth. Lance said if I can make it to what used to be the San Rafael Bridge, Sam will pick me up there.

Dr. Pagent is going to drive me south, along the coast, as far as we can go. I will have to make it the rest of the way on foot. I am leaving tomorrow morning. Sam will meet me the day after.

NOVEMBER 14

I am sitting on a cement pylon that used to be part of the San Rafael-Richmond Bridge. Everything here, and across the channel at Point Richmond, is desolate. Only the snow cover hides the burnt destruction that exists here.

Dr. Pagent and I drove south along the coast yesterday, until we reached a point just north of Jenner. The roadway had crumbled and slipped down the cliffs into the sea. Dr. Pagent maneuvered the jeep up the hillside and around the landslide area.

At the spot where the Russian River used to enter the sea, we drove across a flat sandy barrier. All along the coast we encountered canyons and landslides. Dr. Pagent maneuvered and backtracked until we reached an area north of Stinson Beach. From there south, large sections of land have fallen into the ocean. I gave Dr. Pagent a big hug before she headed back to the north, then I began a cross country trek over Mt. Tamalpais, through Muir Woods and across the leveled waste of Marin County. I reached this spot late last night and found shelter between several large cement blocks. I was glad it was not snowing.

Sam and the fishing boat should be along soon. I have a knot in my stomach. It is fear, apprehension and frustration. I know Frank, dad and Sam are alive and well, but there is no mention of mom, or the girls.

DECEMBER 3

The great California Earthquake, that had been predicted and planned for, had finally struck. It was centered along the San Andreas Fault and measured approximately 8.5. From reports given by military aircraft flying along the coast, massive land damage occurred from San Francisco to Los Angeles. If those areas had been populated, the loss of life would have been in the tens of thousands. There are areas along the coast where entire cities would have disappeared into the ocean. Parts of San Francisco, Monterey, Los Angeles, and San Diego are now under the Pacific Ocean. It is almost as if nature was trying to clean up the mess left by man.

The initial report on New Los Medanos was correct and accurate. Three hundred and fifty-six people died. Among the dead were Shellie, Dr. Bronson, Shawn, and ten of the school kids. Injured included almost everyone in or around the community. Only the citizens who were at the mines, or on outside work crews, were unharmed. Since the quake hit in the early afternoon, most workers were away from the community. A high number of fatalities were among the older members of the community and those too ill to be out working.

Miraculously, mom had taken Jamie and Jackie and had gone to visit Sam at the fishing boat. The quake hit before they reached the river. When the quake had subsided, mom and the girls returned to the college to find Nellie. Mom went through some anxious hours before she found that Nellie had been in between the college building the living quarters when the quake struck. She received some minor cuts and scrapes from falling debris, but was not crushed like Shellie and some of the students.

Rescue efforts at the college were slow and difficult. Snow, cold and lack of heavy equipment made it a long hard task.

By the time I reached New Los Medanos, there was little that I could do. I helped in the recovery of bodies that could be reached under the tons of rubble. I helped in the mass burial of most of the victims. We held separate and private services for Dr. Bronson and Shellie. Donna came here from Marysville for Dr. Bronson's funeral. She is really upset and depressed because of his death.

The last two weeks I have been aiding in the move to the mines. All those who had not already moved, or died in the earthquake, are now moving to the mines to live. The quake had virtually no effect in the mines. Things fell off shelves, cement cracked in places, and a few pipes broke, but nothing major. By the end of the month all the survivors from New Los Medanos will be living and working in the mines. The college area will be totally abandoned. The only locals living outside the mines will be a group of thirteen men and women who have built living quarters near the river. They are the crews of the fishing boats.

DECEMBER 6

Operation Groundhog. The plan developed for war survivors to live through nuclear winter. The state, the country, and most likely the world, are experiencing cold and snow. All the dirt and ash sent into the atmosphere by the exploding missile warheads are blocking out the warmth and ultraviolet light of the sun.

I am sitting outside the main entrance to the mine complex. It snowed heavily last night. It will probably snow every night for a long time. Some scientists say it could last years. Some have even predicted an Ice Age. The most pessimistic have said that humanity is doomed.

The fragmented and disenfranchised government, military, and scientific leadership is trying to save and support the pockets of humanity scattered across this country. Operation Groundhog is their hastily designed plan. Everywhere, survivors are digging in. Moving into underground buildings, complexes, and communities. Our group here was fortunate, because we already have an underground area. In the time most other survivor groups have been moving underground, workers here have been making the mines livable. We will be more prepared and comfortable than many survivor groups. Perhaps, in a few years, like groundhogs, we can move back out into the sunlight and see our own shadows again.

DECEMBER 23

We buried Donna today. Night before last she went to her living quarters and gave herself a massive injection of barbiturates. She left a simple note that said in part:

".....and the pain of having lost everything I love, twice, is more than I can bare. I take the easy way out, rather than face anymore pain."

After the funeral outside, I stayed by the grave until long after everyone had gone back into the mines. I find myself making more and more excuses to go out. I prefer the cold and frosty air to the regulated warmth and manufactured odors of the mines. Maybe I'm acquiring claustrophobia.

It has been almost a year since the war. It has been almost as long since I started keeping this diary. I still have the feeling that no one will ever read it, so why write. This will be my last entry.

As long as there are periodic shipments of food, we can survive in these mines indefinitely. We have filtered air, drinkable water, and hydroponic gardens. We have heat and artificial light.

For my younger sisters, this is fine. This is their world. They are post war babies who have nothing to compare this world to. Nellie is a little different. She has memories of a better world, but she can adapt to this world by having hope for a better future. My father is dying. By his own wish, he is working tirelessly, so he won't linger, or suffer. My mother spends most of her time fussing about nothing, over my sisters and I. She creates work and diversions for herself. Most of the time she is totally depressed. It it weren't for the girls, I think she would follow Donna's lead.

From post war disease, moving to other areas, and the earthquake, the population in the mines is just under eight hundred. The attitude of the survivors left is resolute. They want to live and rebuild the world. It is truly survival of the fittest.

I am not sure where I fit in. I want to live, but I'm not sure for what. I am helping Nellie teach, but I do not feel it is purposeful. The work is not as meaningful as it should be. I would like to find a way to return to the coast, but I cannot leave my family. I stay close to Frank and the radio. I stay in contact with Lance, Dr. Pagent, Bill and Dave. Each time I talk to them I hear about their important work and projects.

I am committed to staying here as long as I can. Eventually, I will leave. Perhaps after dad dies. Maybe when, and if, the weather gets better. Maybe never. Maybe I'll get use to living in the ground.

I keep having this nagging thought, that all the dead people went to heaven, and we, the living, are in hell.

The End

APPENDIX – 1

DISCUSSION TOPICS AND QUESTIONS

We have long lived with the possibility of nuclear destruction and the history of major natural disasters. How individuals react in times of major crisis is important for their personal survival and possibly for the survival of others. The following Topics And Questions give readers of this book an opportunity to do a little "Critical Thinking" on the subject of survival. The Topics And Questions cut across several curriculum areas considered important in our educational systems. These Topics And Questions can be used by Teachers, Parents, Student Groups, or Civic Organizations, to stimulate discussion, create writing projects, or increase personal self knowledge.

This is not a "Doomsday" book. It is a fictional account of how terrible and devastating a nuclear war, or any other worldwide disaster, could be. It is written by a teacher, with young people in mind, but it is for all readers, of all ages. It is for all people who have never considered the possibility of a global holocaust and its immediate and long term effects.

SCIENCE

When discussing the topic of Nuclear War, there are a great many scientific aspects that should be considered. Chemistry, Nuclear Physics, Ecology, and Biological Science must all be discussed. First, we must attempt to understand how nuclear weapons work and differ from conventional weapons. Secondly, all humans must be aware of the short and long term effects of nuclear weapons.

QUESTIONS

1) Is there a difference between Atomic Bombs and Nuclear Bombs?

2) What is Nuclear Fission? Fusion?

3) What are the immediate effects of a 10 megaton nuclear device at ground zero? At 1 mile? At 5 miles? At 10 miles? At 25 miles?

4) Are the effects of nuclear weapons increased by multiple detonations?

5) What is Nuclear Fallout? How does it effect humans? Plants? Animals?

6) How long does Fallout last? Can you survive exposure to Fallout?

7) What are the long term effects of exposure to Fallout? Can it be measured, monitored, or controlled?

8) What are mutations? How does Nuclear Radiation effect mutations?

9) What is Nuclear Winter? How does Nuclear Winter differ from the "Greenhouse Effect"?

10) Could the Human Race survive an all out Nuclear War?

ETHICS AND VALUES

In any discussion of survival, whether from nuclear holocaust or natural disaster, we must examine our personal values. First, we must look at whether or not we took an active part in helping to prevent or prepare for a major catastrophe, or did we stand idly by and allow others to make our choices and decisions for us. Second, would we want to survive a major catastrophe or holocaust, knowing that nothing would ever be the same again. Finally, how is our personal value system going to change in order to be a survivor in a devastated world. Society. Environment.

QUESTIONS

1) What would you do to prevent Nuclear War? What can you do?

2) Are you and your family prepared to survive a Nuclear War? A major Earthquake? Flood? Plague? Terrorist Attack?

3) Do you assume that there is a government agency that is doing all the planning, preparing and worrying, about world catastrophe, for you? Do you know? Do you care?

4) In the event of a worldwide holocaust, natural or man made, would you want to survive?

5) Can you imagine our world after a major global disaster? Our form of government? Living conditions?

SURVIVAL

An individual may not have the choice of surviving a cataclysmic world disaster. You may simply wake up someday to find yourself facing a new reality. You could lie down and wait for death, or you could go out and attempt to be a survivor. What does a survivor do?

QUESTIONS

1) What would be your first requirements for survival? Where would you look to find what you need?

2) Would you want to be separate from other survivors? Would you want to join the other survivors? Would you want to help others?

3) What skills do you have to be a survivor? What skills could you offer others? Medical? Carpentry? Farmer? Mechanical?

4) Would you go along with majority rule? Would you accept the rules and laws of a new government or leadership?

5) Are you a leader or a follower? Would you try to help rebuild the world, or simply do whatever you were expected to do by others?

6) What elements of our present society would you try to keep? Government? Religion? Customs? Folklore? Education? Music? Art? Science?

7) How would you feel about the loss of family members, friends, relatives? How would you deal with the loss?

8) If others had something you needed to survive, that is, water, food, shelter; but would not share, what would you do? How far would you go to survive?

9) Do you think you would be interested in how people are surviving in other places? Would you consider traveling to other places to find food, water, shelter, companionship?

10) Can you imagine what we would eat? Where we might live? What we would use for money? How we would deal with illness, disease, or criminals?

GOVERNMENT

Every country on the planet today has some form of government. Some differ from others a little, some differ a lot. All governments, whether religiously motivated, or ideologically founded, exist for the well being of the populations they serve. Many forms of government have come and gone, some lasting longer than others. In the event of a worldwide cataclysm, the surviving members of various societies would have to create, or recreate, some form of government or rules.

QUESTIONS

1) If you were a survivor of a worldwide disaster, what form of government, or rule, would you want? Dictatorship? Monarchy? Democratic? Socialist?

2) Do you believe survivors around the world would recreate the same form of government they had before a disaster? Even though that government may have been responsible for the disaster?

3) Do rules make us civilized? Do we have to have laws or rules in order to survive?

4) Who would be our leaders after a global holocaust? How would we select our new leaders if none of the old leaders survived?

5) Who would enforce the will, or laws, of a new government? Who would select the enforcers? How would they be paid?

APPENDIX - 2

RELATED READING LIST

NUCLEAR WAR THREAT

Title: If You Give A Damn About Life
Author: Harold Freeman; 1985
Publisher: Dodd, Mead; New York

Title: No Reason To Talk About It: Families Confront
             Nuclear War
Author: David S. Greenwald; 1987
Publisher: Norton; New York

Title: Nuclear Fear: A History Of Images
Author: Spencer R. Weart; 1988
Publisher: Harvard University Press; Cambridge,
             MA

Title: A Guide To Radiation Protection
Author: Craig J. Roberts; 1976
Publisher: Wiley; New York

Title: Radiation Hazards And Protection
Author: David E. Barnes; 1958
Publisher: Newnes

SURVIVAL

Title: Extinction Of The Species
Author: Paul Erlich; 1981
Publisher: Random House; New York

Title: A Guide To Life After Doomsday
Author: Bruce Clayton; 1980
Publisher: Dial Press; New York

Title: The Day After World War III
Author: Ed Zuckerman; 1984
Publisher: Viking; New York

WORLD WAR III

Title: The Strangelove Legacy
Author: Phylis La Farge; 1987
Publisher: Harper, Rowe; New York

Title: Missile Envy: The Arms Race
Author: Helen Caldicott; 1986
Publisher: Bantam Books; New York

Title: Chemical And Biological Warfare
Author: L.B. Taylor; 1985
Publisher: Watts; New York

Title: Understanding Weapons In A Nuclear Arsenal
Author: Kosta Tsipis; 1983
Publisher: Simon, Schuster; New York

Title: First Strike: Pentagon Strategy
Author: Robert C. Aldridge; 1983
Publisher: Southend Press; Boston, MA

NUCLEAR WINTER

Title: Hiroshima To Nuclear Winter
Author: Laurence P. Pringle; 1985
Publisher: Enslow; Hillside, New Jersey

Title: Nuclear War, Nuclear Winter
Author: Gene B. Williams; 1987
Publisher: F. Watts; New York

SYNTHETIC FUELS

Title: Driving Without Gas
Author: John Ware Lincoln; 1980
Publisher: Garden Way; Charlotte, VT

Title: Make Your Own Fuel
Author: Jerry Wilkerson; 1979
Publisher: Young Publishers Inc.

Title: <u>Methanol And Other Ways...</u>
Author: John Ware Lincoln; 1976
Publisher: Garden Way; Charlotte, VT

MUTATIONS

Title: <u>Nuclear War - Environmental</u>
Author: Lydia Dotto; 1986
Publisher: For Scope & ICSU; Chichester, New York

Title: <u>How Wildlife Survives Natural Disaster</u>
Author: Sarah Riedman; 1977
Publisher: McKay; New York

Title: <u>Biology Of The Cockroach</u>
Author: David M. Guthrie; 1968
Publisher: Edward Arnold; London

Title: <u>California Insects</u>
Author: Jerry A. Powell; 1979
Publisher: U.C. Berkeley Press; Berkeley, CA

Title: <u>Ecology Of Invasions By Animals</u>
Author: Charles S. Elton; 1958
Author: Charles S. Elton; 1958
Publisher: Not Available

CONTRA COSTA COAL MINES

Title: <u>Move Of The Nortonville Coalminers</u>
Author: Jacqueline Byer Dial; 1980
Publisher: J.B. Dial; Brentwood, CA

Title: <u>Coal Mines Of The West Coast</u>
Author: W.A. Goodyear; 1877
Publisher: U.S. Government

Title: <u>Mt. Diablo And Its Coal Mines</u>
Author: East Diablo Historical Assn; 1986
Publisher: East Diablo Historical Assn.; Contra Costa County, CA

CIVIL DEFENSE PREPAREDNESS

Title: Contra Costa County Civil Defense Plan
Author: Contra Costa County; 1960
Publisher: Contra Costa County; Martinez, CA

Title: Emergency Plan: Civil Defense
Author: Contra Costa County Administrator; 1973
Publisher: Contra Costa County; Martinez, CA

Title: Statistical Abstract: Civil Defense
Author: Smith and Associates; 1973
Publisher: Association Of Bay Area Governments; San Francisco, CA

FOOD FOR SURVIVORS

Title: Grow More Without Soil
Author: James D. Taylor; 1983
Publisher: Parkside Press; Santa Ana, CA

Title: Hydroponics For The Home Gardener
Author: Stewart Kenyon; 1979
Publisher: Van Nostrand Reinhold; New York

Title: Sea Life Of The Pacific Northwest
Author: Stefani Hewlett; 1976
Publisher: McGraw Hill; Ryerson, New York

COMMUNICATIONS

Title: Complete Shortwave Listeners Handbook
Author: Hank Bennett; 1986
Publisher: Tab Books; Blue Ridge Summit, PA